AND FOUR TO GO

Christmas Party
Easter Parade
Fourth of July Picnic
Murder Is No Joke

Four memorable mysteries prove what Nero Wolfe
and Archie Goodwin have always suspected . . .
MURDER NEVER TAKES A HOLIDAY.

A NERO WOLFE NOVEL

AND FOUR TO GO

BY REX STOUT

BANTAM BOOKS · TORONTO · NEW YORK · LONDON

❦

AND FOUR TO GO

*A Bantam Book | published by arrangement with
The Viking Press, Inc.*

PRINTING HISTORY

*Viking edition published July 1958
Mystery Guild edition published August 1958
Bantam edition published November 1959
2nd printing .... August 1967
3rd printing .... October 1967
New Bantam edition published December 1974
2nd printing .... April 1981*

ISBN 0-553-14452-9

Published simultaneously in the United States and Canada

PRINTED IN THE UNITED STATES OF AMERICA

11 10 9 8 7 6 5 4 3 2

CONTENTS

Christmas Party   1
Easter Parade   65
Fourth of July Picnic   111
Murder Is No Joke   155

Christmas
Party

I

"I'm sorry, sir," I said. I tried to sound sorry. "But I told you two days ago, Monday, that I had a date for Friday afternoon, and you said all right. So I'll drive you to Long Island Saturday or Sunday."

Nero Wolfe shook his head. "That won't do. Mr. Thompson's ship docks Friday morning, and he will be at Mr. Hewitt's place only until Saturday noon, when he leaves for New Orleans. As you know, he is the best hybridizer in England, and I am grateful to Mr. Hewitt for inviting me to spend a few hours with him. As I remember, the drive takes about an hour and a half, so we should leave at twelve-thirty."

I decided to count ten, and swiveled my chair, facing my desk, so as to have privacy for it. As usual when we have no important case going, we had been getting on each other's nerves for a week, and I admit I was a little touchy, but his taking it for granted like that was a little too much. When I had finished the count I turned my head, to where he was perched on his throne behind his desk, and darned if he hadn't gone back to his book, making it plain that he regarded it as settled. That was much too much. I swiveled my chair to confront him.

"I really am sorry," I said, not trying to sound sorry, "but I have to keep that date Friday afternoon. It's a Christmas party at the office of Kurt Bottweill—you remember him, we did a job for him a few months ago, the stolen tapestries. You may not remember a member of his staff named Margot Dickey, but I do. I have been seeing her some, and I promised her I'd go to the party. We never have a Christmas office party here. As for going to Long Island, your idea

3

that a car is a death trap if I'm not driving it is unsound. You can take a taxi, or hire a Baxter man, or get Saul Panzer to drive you."

Wolfe had lowered his book. "I hope to get some useful information from Mr. Thompson, and you will take notes."

"Not if I'm not there. Hewitt's secretary knows orchid terms as well as I do. So do you."

I admit those last three words were a bit strong, but he shouldn't have gone back to his book. His lips tightened. "Archie. How many times in the past year have I asked you to drive me somewhere?"

"If you call it asking, maybe eighteen or twenty."

"Not excessive, surely. If my feeling that you alone are to be trusted at the wheel of a car is an aberration, I have it. We will leave for Mr. Hewitt's place Friday at twelve-thirty."

So there we were. I took a breath, but I didn't need to count ten again. If he was to be taught a lesson, and he certainly needed one, luckily I had in my possession a document that would make it good. Reaching to my inside breast pocket, I took out a folded sheet of paper.

"I didn't intend," I told him, "to spring this on you until tomorrow, or maybe even later, but I guess it will have to be now. Just as well, I suppose."

I left my chair, unfolded the paper, and handed it to him. He put his book down to take it, gave it a look, shot a glance at me, looked at the paper again, and let it drop on his desk.

He snorted. "Pfui. What flummery is this?"

"No flummery. As you see, it's a marriage license for Archie Goodwin and Margot Dickey. It cost me two bucks. I could be mushy about it, but I won't. I will only say that if I am hooked at last, it took an expert. She intends to spread the tidings at the Christmas office party, and of course I have to be there. When you announce you have caught a fish it helps to have the fish present in person. Frankly, I would prefer to drive you to Long Island, but it can't be done."

The effect was all I could have asked. He gazed at me through narrowed eyes long enough to count

4

eleven, then picked up the document and gazed at it. He flicked it to the edge of the desk as if it were crawling with germs, and focused on me again.

"You are deranged," he said evenly and distinctly. "Sit down."

I nodded. "I suppose," I agreed, remaining upright, "it's a form of madness, but so what if I've got it? Like what Margot was reading to me the other night—some poet, I think it was some Greek—'O love, resistless in thy might, thou triumphest even—'"

"Shut up and sit down!"

"Yes, sir." I didn't move. "But we're not rushing it. We haven't set the date, and there'll be plenty of time to decide on adjustments. You may not want me here any more, but that's up to you. As far as I'm concerned, I would like to stay. My long association with you has had its flaws, but I would hate to end it. The pay is okay, especially if I get a raise the first of the year, which is a week from Monday. I have grown to regard this old brownstone as my home, although you own it and although there are two creaky boards in the floor of my room. I appreciate working for the greatest private detective in the free world, no matter how eccentric he is. I appreciate being able to go up to the plant rooms whenever I feel like it and look at ten thousand orchids, especially the odontoglossums. I fully appreciate—"

"Sit down!"

"I'm too worked up to sit. I fully appreciate Fritz's cooking. I like the billiard table in the basement. I like West Thirty-fifth Street. I like the one-way glass panel in the front door. I like this rug I'm standing on. I like your favorite color, yellow. I have told Margot all this, and more, including the fact that you are allergic to women. We have discussed it, and we think it may be worth trying, say for a month, when we get back from the honeymoon. My room could be our bedroom, and the other room on that floor could be our living room. There are plenty of closets. We could eat with you, as I have been, or we could eat up there, as you prefer. If the trial works out, new furniture or redecorating would be up to us.

5

She will keep her job with Kurt Bottweill, so she wouldn't be here during the day, and since he's an interior decorator we would get things wholesale. Of course we merely suggest this for your consideration. It's your house."

I picked up my marriage license, folded it, and returned it to my pocket.

His eyes had stayed narrow and his lips tight. "I don't believe it," he growled. "What about Miss Rowan?"

"We won't drag Miss Rowan into this," I said stiffly.

"What about the thousands of others you dally with?"

"Not thousands. Not even a thousand. I'll have to look up 'dally.' They'll get theirs, as Margot has got hers. As you see, I'm deranged only up to a point. I realize—"

"Sit down."

"No, sir. I know this will have to be discussed, but right now you're stirred up and it would be better to wait for a day or two, or maybe more. By Saturday the idea of a woman in the house may have you boiling even worse than you are now, or it may have cooled you down to a simmer. If the former, no discussion will be needed. If the latter, you may decide it's worth a try. I hope you do."

I turned and walked out.

In the hall I hesitated. I could have gone up to my room and phoned from there, but in his present state it was quite possible he would listen in from his desk, and the call I wanted to make was personal. So I got my hat and coat from the rack, let myself out, descended the stoop steps, walked to the drugstore on Ninth Avenue, found the booth unoccupied, and dialed a number. In a moment a musical little voice —more a chirp than a voice—was in my ear.

"Kurt Bottweill's studio, good morning."

"The is Archie Goodwin, Cherry. May I speak to Margot?"

"Why, certainly. Just a moment."

It was a fairly long moment. Then another voice. "Archie, darling!"

6

"Yes, my own. I've got it."

"I knew you could!"

"Sure, I can do anything. Not only that, you said up to a hundred bucks, and I thought I would have to part with twenty at least, but it only took five. And not only that, but it's on me, because I've already had my money's worth of fun out of it, and more. I'll tell you about it when I see you. Shall I send it up by messenger?"

"No, I don't think—I'd better come and get it. Where are you?"

"In a phone booth. I'd just as soon not go back to the office right now because Mr. Wolfe wants to be alone to boil, so how about the Tulip Bar at the Churchill in twenty minutes? I feel like buying you a drink."

"I feel like buying *you* a drink!"

She should, since I was treating her to a marriage license.

II

When, at three o'clock Friday afternoon, I wriggled out of the taxi at the curb in front of the four-story building in the East Sixties, it was snowing. If it kept up, New York might have an off-white Christmas.

During the two days that had passed since I got my money's worth from the marriage license, the atmosphere around Wolfe's place had not been very seasonable. If we had had a case going, frequent and sustained communication would have been unavoidable, but without one there was nothing that absolutely had to be said, and we said it. Our handling of that trying period showed our true natures. At table, for instance, I was polite and reserved, and spoke, when speaking seemed necessary, in low and cultured tones. When Wolfe spoke he either snapped or barked. Neither of us mentioned the state of bliss I was headed for, or the adjustments that would have to be made, or my Friday date with my fiancée, or his trip to Long Island. But he arranged it somehow, for precisely at twelve-thirty on Friday a black limousine drew up in front of the house, and Wolfe, with the brim of his old black hat turned down and the collar of his new gray overcoat turned up for the snow, descended the stoop, stood massively, the mountain of him, on the bottom step until the uniformed chauffeur had opened the door, and crossed the sidewalk and climbed in. I watched it from above, from a window of my room.

I admit I was relieved and felt better. He had unquestionably needed a lesson and I didn't regret giving him one, but if he had passed up a chance for an orchid powwow with the best hybridizer in England I would never have heard the last of it. I went down to the kitchen and ate lunch with Fritz, who was so upset by the atmosphere that he forgot to put the lemon juice in the soufflé. I wanted to console him by telling him that everything would be rosy by Christmas, only three days off, but of course that wouldn't do.

I had a notion to toss a coin to decide whether I would have a look at the new exhibit of dinosaurs at the Natural History Museum or go to the Bottweill party, but I was curious to know how Margot was making out with the license, and also how the other Bottweill personnel were making out with each other. It was surprising that they were still making out at all. Cherry Quon's position in the setup was apparently minor, since she functioned chiefly as a receptionist and phone-answerer, but I had seen her black eyes dart daggers at Margot Dickey, who should have been clear out of her reach. I had gathered that it was Margot who was mainly relied upon to wrangle prospective customers into the corral, that Bottweill himself put them under the spell, and that Alfred Kiernan's part was to make sure that before the spell wore off an order got signed on the dotted line.

Of course that wasn't all. The order had to be filled, and that was handled, under Bottweill's supervision, by Emil Hatch in the workshop. Also funds were required to buy ingredients, and they were furnished by a specimen named Mrs. Perry Porter Jerome. Margot had told me that Mrs. Jerome would be at the party and would bring her son Leo, whom I had never met. According to Margot, Leo, who had no connection with the Bottweill business or any other business, devoted his time to two important activities: getting enough cash from his mother to keep going as a junior playboy, and stopping the flow of cash to Bottweill, or at least slowing it down.

It was quite a tangle, an interesting exhibit of bipeds alive and kicking, and, deciding it promised more entertainment than the dead dinosaurs, I took a taxi to the East Sixties.

The ground floor of the four-story building, formerly a de luxe double-width residence, was now a beauty shop. The second floor was a real-estate office. The third floor was Kurt Bottweill's workshop, and on top was his studio. From the vestibule I took the do-it-yourself elevator to the top, opened the door, and stepped out into the glossy gold-leaf elegance I had first seen some months back, when Bottweill had hired Wolfe to find out who had swiped some tapestries. On that first visit I had decided that the only big difference between chrome modern and Bottweill gold-leaf modern was the color, and I still thought so. Not even skin deep; just a two-hundred-thousandth of an inch deep. But on the panels and racks and furniture frames it gave the big skylighted studio quite a tone, and the rugs and drapes and pictures, all modern, joined in. It would have been a fine den for a blind millionaire.

"Archie!" a voice called. "Come and help us sample!"

It was Margot Dickey. In a far corner was a gold-leaf bar, some eight feet long, and she was at it on a gold-leaf stool. Cherry Quon and Alfred Kiernan were with her, also on stools, and behind the bar was Santa Claus, pouring from a champagne bottle. It was certainly a modern touch to have Santa Claus tend bar, but there was nothing modern about his costume. He was strictly traditional, cut, color, size, mask, and all, except that the hand grasping the champagne bottle wore a white glove. I assumed, crossing to them over the thick rugs, that that was a touch of Bottweill elegance, and didn't learn until later how wrong I was.

They gave me the season's greetings, and Santa Claus poured a glass of bubbles for me. No gold leaf on the glass. I was glad I had come. To drink champagne with a blonde at one elbow and a brunette at the other gives a man a sense of well-being, and those two were fine specimens—the tall, slender Margot relaxed, all curves, on the stool, and little slant-eyed black-eyed Cherry Quon, who came only up to my collar when standing, sitting with her spine as straight as a plumb line, yet not stiff. I thought Cherry worthy of notice not only as a statuette, though she was highly decorative, but as a possible source of new light on human relations. Margot had told me that her father was half Chinese and half Indian—not American Indian—and her mother was Dutch.

I said that apparently I had come too early, but Alfred Kiernan said no, the others were around and would be in shortly. He added that it was a pleasant surprise to see me, as it was just a little family gathering and he hadn't known others had been invited. Kiernan, whose title was business manager, had not liked a certain step I had taken when I was hunting the tapestries, and he still didn't, but an Irishman at a Christmas party likes everybody. My impression was that he really was pleased, so I was too. Margot said she had invited me, and Kiernan patted her on the arm and said that if she hadn't he would. About my age and fully as handsome, he was the kind who can pat the arm of a queen or a president's wife without making eyebrows go up.

He said we needed another sample and turned to the bartender. "Mr. Claus, we'll try the Veuve Clicquot." To us: "Just like Kurt to provide different brands. No monotony for Kurt." To the bartender: "May I call you by your first name, Santy?"

"Certainly, sir," Santa Claus told him from behind the mask in a thin falsetto that didn't match his size. As he stopped and came up with a bottle a door at the left opened and two men entered. One of them, Emil Hatch, I had met before. When briefing Wolfe on the tapestries and telling us about his staff, Bottweill had called Margot Dickey his contact woman, Cherry Quon his handy girl, and Emil Hatch his pet wizard, and when I met Hatch I found that he both looked the part and acted it. He wasn't much taller than Cherry Quon and skinny, and something had either pushed his left shoulder down or his right shoulder up, making him lopsided, and he had a sour face, a sour voice, and a sour taste.

When the stranger was named to me as Leo Jerome, that placed him. I was acquainted with his mother, Mrs. Perry Porter Jerome. She was a widow and an angel—that is, Kurt Bottweill's angel. During the

11

investigation she had talked as if the tapestries belonged to her, but that might have only been her manners, of which she had plenty. I could have made guesses about her personal relations with Bottweill, but hadn't bothered. I have enough to do to handle my own personal relations without wasting my brain power on other people's. As for her son Leo, he must have got his physique from his father—tall, bony, big-eared and long-armed. He was probably approaching thirty, below Kiernan but above Margot and Cherry.

When he shoved in between Cherry and me, giving me his back, and Emil Hatch had something to tell Kiernan, sour no doubt, I touched Margot's elbow and she slid off the stool and let herself be steered across to a divan which had been covered with designs by Euclid in six or seven colors. We stood looking down at it.

"Mighty pretty," I said, "but nothing like as pretty as you. If only that license were real! I can get a real one for two dollars. What do you say?"

"*You!*" she said scornfully. "You wouldn't marry Miss Universe if she came on her knees with a billion dollars."

"I dare her to try it. Did it work?"

"Perfect. Simply perfect."

"Then you're ditching me?"

"Yes, Archie darling. But I'll be a sister to you."

"I've got a sister. I want the license back for a souvenir, and anyway I don't want it kicking around. I could be hooked for forgery. You can mail it to me, once my own."

"No, I can't. He tore it up."

"The hell he did. Where are the pieces?"

"Gone. He put them in his wastebasket. Will you come to the wedding?"

"What wastebasket where?"

"The gold one by his desk in his office. Last evening after dinner. Will you come to the wedding?"

"I will not. My heart is bleeding. So will Mr. Wolfe's—and by the way, I'd better get out of here. I'm not going to stand around and sulk."

"You won't have to. He won't know I've told you, and anyway, you wouldn't be expected— Here he comes!"

She darted off to the bar and I headed that way. Through the door on the left appeared Mrs. Perry Porter Jerome, all of her, plump and plushy, with folds of mink trying to keep up as she breezed in. As she approached, those on stools left them and got onto their feet, but that courtesy could have been as much for her companion as for her. She was the angel, but Kurt Bottweill was the boss. He stopped five paces short of the bar, extended his arms as far as they would go, and sang out, "Merry Christmas, all my blessings! Merry merry merry!"

I still hadn't labeled him. My first impression, months ago, had been that he was one of them, but that had been wrong. He was a man all right, but the question was what kind. About average in height, round but not pudgy, maybe forty-two or -three, his fine black hair slicked back so that he looked balder than he was, he was nothing great to look at, but he had something, not only for women but for men too. Wolfe had once invited him to stay for dinner, and they had talked about the scrolls from the Dead Sea. I had seen him twice at baseball games. His label would have to wait.

As I joined them at the bar, where Santa Claus was pouring Mumms Cordon Rouge, Bottweill squinted at me a moment and then grinned. "Goodwin! You here? Good! Edith, your pet sleuth!"

Mrs. Perry Porter Jerome, reaching for a glass, stopped her hand to look at me. "Who asked you?" she demanded, then went on, with no room for a reply, "Cherry, I suppose. Cherry *is* a blessing. Leo, quit tugging at me. Very well, take it. It's warm in here." She let her son pull her coat off, then reached for a glass. By the time Leo got back from depositing the mink on the divan we all had glasses, and when he had his we raised them, and our eyes went to Bottweill.

His eyes flashed around. "There are times," he said, "when love takes over. There are times—"

13

"Wait a minute," Alfred Kiernan cut in. "You enjoy it too. You don't like this stuff."

"I can stand a sip, Al."

"But you won't enjoy it. Wait." Kiernan put his glass on the bar and marched to the door on the left and on out. In five seconds he was back, with a bottle in his hand, and as he rejoined us and asked Santa Claus for a glass I saw the Pernod label. He pulled the cork, which had been pulled before, filled the glass halfway, and held it out to Bottweill. "There," he said. "That will make it unanimous."

"Thanks, Al." Bottweill took it. "My secret public vice." He raised the glass. "I repeat, there are times when love takes over. (Santa Claus, where is yours? But I suppose you can't drink through that mask.) There are times when all the little demons disappear down their ratholes, and ugliness itself takes on the shape of beauty; when the darkest corner is touched by light; when the coldest heart feels the glow of warmth; when the trumpet call of good will and good cheer drowns out all the Babel of mean little noises. This is such a time. Merry Christmas! Merry merry merry!"

I was ready to touch glasses, but both the angel and the boss steered theirs to their lips, so I and the others followed suit. I thought Bottweill's eloquence deserved more than a sip, so I took a healthy gulp, and from the corner of my eye I saw that he was doing likewise with the Pernod. As I lowered the glass my eyes went to Mrs. Jerome, as she spoke.

"That was lovely," she declared. "Simply lovely. I must write it down and have it printed. That part about the trumpet call—*Kurt!* What is it? *Kurt!*"

He had dropped the glass and was clutching his throat with both hands. As I moved he turned loose of his throat, thrust his arms out, and let out a yell. I think he yelled "*Merry!*" but I wasn't really listening. Others started for him too, but my reflexes were better trained for emergencies than any of theirs, so I got him first. As I got my arms around him he started choking and gurgling, and a spasm went over him

14

from head to foot that nearly loosened my grip. They were making noises, but no screams, and someone was clawing at my arm. As I was telling them to get back and give me room, he was suddenly a dead weight, and I almost went down with him and might have if Kiernan hadn't grabbed his arm.

I called, "Get a doctor!" and Cherry ran to a table where there was a gold-leaf phone. Kiernan and I let Bottweill down on the rug. He was out, breathing fast and hard, but as I was straightening his head his breathing slowed down and foam showed on his lips. Mrs. Jerome was commanding us, "Do something, do something!"

There was nothing to do and I knew it. While I was holding onto him I had got a whiff of his breath, and now, kneeling, I leaned over to get my nose an inch from his, and I knew that smell, and it takes a big dose to hit that quick and hard. Kiernan was loosening Bottweill's tie and collar. Cherry Quon called to us that she had tried a doctor and couldn't get him and was trying another. Margot was squatting at Bottweill's feet, taking his shoes off, and I could have told her she might as well let him die with his boots on but didn't. I had two fingers on his wrist and my other hand inside his shirt, and could feel him going.

When I could feel nothing I abandoned the chest and wrist, took his hand, which was a fist, straightened the middle finger, and pressed its nail with my thumbtip until it was white. When I removed my thumb the nail stayed white. Dropping the hand, I yanked a little cluster of fibers from the rug, told Kiernan not to move, placed the fibers against Bottweill's nostrils, fastened my eyes on them, and held my breath for thirty seconds. The fibers didn't move.

I stood up and spoke. "His heart has stopped and he's not breathing. If a doctor came within three minutes and washed out his stomach with chemicals he wouldn't have with him, there might be one chance in a thousand. As it is—"

"Can't you *do* something?" Mrs. Jerome squawked.

"Not for him, no. I'm not an officer of the law,

15

but I'm a licensed detective, and I'm supposed to
know how to act in these circumstances, and I'll get it
if I don't follow the rules. Of course—"

"*Do something!*" Mrs. Jerome squawked.

Kiernan's voice came from behind me. "He's
dead."

I didn't turn to ask what test he had used. "Of
course," I told them, "his drink was poisoned. Until
the police come no one will touch anything, especially
the bottle of Pernod, and no one will leave this room.
You will—"

I stopped dead. Then I demanded, "Where is
Santa Claus?"

Their heads turned to look at the bar. No bartender. On the chance that it had been too much for him,
I pushed between Leo Jerome and Emil Hatch to step
to the end of the bar, but he wasn't on the floor either.

I wheeled. "Did anyone see him go?"

They hadn't. Hatch said, "He didn't take the elevator. I'm sure he didn't. He must have—" He started
off.

I blocked him. "You stay here. I'll take a look.
Kiernan, phone the police. Spring seven-three-one-
hundred."

I made for the door on the left and passed
through, pulling it shut as I went, and was in Bottweill's office, which I had seen before. It was one-
fourth the size of the studio, and much more subdued,
but was by no means squalid. I crossed to the far end,
saw through the glass panel that Bottweill's private elevator wasn't there, and pressed the button. A clank
and a whirr came from inside the shaft, and it was
coming. When it was up and had jolted to a stop I
opened the door, and there on the floor was Santa
Claus, but only the outside of him. He had molted.
Jacket, breeches, mask, wig . . . I didn't check to see
if it was all there because I had another errand and
not much time for it.

Propping the elevator door open with a chair, I
went and circled around Bottweill's big gold-leaf desk
to his gold-leaf wastebasket. It was one-third full.
Bending, I started to paw, decided that was inefficient,

16

picked it up and dumped it, and began tossing things back in one by one. Some of the items were torn pieces of paper, but none of them came from a marriage license. When I had finished I stayed down a moment, squatting, wondering if I had hurried too much and possibly missed it, and I might have gone through it again if I hadn't heard a faint noise from the studio that sounded like the elevator door opening. I went to the door to the studio and opened it, and as I crossed the sill two uniformed cops were deciding whether to give their first glance to the dead or the living.

III

Three hours later we were seated, more or less in a group, and my old friend and foe, Sergeant Purley Stebbins of Homicide, stood surveying us, his square jaw jutting and his big burly frame erect.

He spoke. "Mr. Kiernan and Mr. Hatch will be taken to the District Attorney's office for further questioning. The rest of you can go for the present, but you will keep yourselves available at the addresses you have given. Before you go I want to ask you again, here together, about the man who was here as Santa Claus. You have all claimed you know nothing about him. Do you still claim that?"

It was twenty minutes to seven. Some two dozen city employees—medical examiner, photographer, fingerprinters, meat-basket bearers, the whole kaboodle—had finished the on-the-scene routine, including private interviews with the eyewitnesses. I had made the highest score, having had sessions with Stebbins, a precinct man, and Inspector Cramer, who had departed around five o'clock to organize the hunt for Santa Claus.

"I'm not objecting," Kiernan told Stebbins, "to going to the District Attorney's office. I'm not objecting to anything. But we've told you all we can, I know I have. It seems to me your job is to find him."

"Do you mean to say," Mrs. Jerome demanded, "that no one knows anything at all about him?"

"So they say," Purley told her. "No one even knew there was going to be a Santa Claus, so they say. He was brought to this room by Bottweill, about a quarter to three, from his office. The idea is that Bott-

18

weill himself had arranged for him, and he came up in the private elevator and put on the costume in Bottweill's office. You may as well know there is some corroboration of that. We have found out where the costume came from—Burleson's on Forty-sixth Street. Bottweill phoned them yesterday afternoon and ordered it sent here, marked personal. Miss Quon admits receiving the package and taking it to Bottweill in his office."

For a cop, you never just state a fact, or report it or declare it or say it. You admit it.

"We are also," Purley admitted, "covering agencies which might have supplied a man to act Santa Claus, but that's a big order. If Bottweill got a man through an agency there's no telling what he got. If it was a man with a record, when he saw trouble coming he beat it. With everybody's attention on Bottweill, he sneaked out, got his clothes, whatever he had taken off, in Bottweill's office, and went down in the elevator he had come up in. He shed the costume on the way down and after he was down, and left it in the elevator. If that was it, if he was just a man Bottweill hired, he wouldn't have had any reason to kill him—and besides, he wouldn't have known that Bottweill's only drink was Pernod, and he wouldn't have known where the poison was."

"Also," Emil Hatch said, sourer than ever, "if he was just hired for the job he was a damn fool to sneak out. He might have known he'd be found. So he wasn't just hired. He was someone who knew Bottweill, and knew about the Pernod and the poison, and had some good reason for wanting to kill him. You're wasting your time on the agencies."

Stebbins lifted his heavy broad shoulders and dropped them. "We waste most of our time, Mr. Hatch. Maybe he was too scared to think. I just want you to understand that if we find him and that's how Bottweill got him, it's going to be hard to believe that he put poison in that bottle, but somebody did. I want you to understand that so you'll understand why you are all to be available at the addresses you have given. Don't make any mistake about that."

"Do you mean," Mrs. Jerome demanded, "that we are under suspicion? That *I* and *my son* are under suspicion?"

Purley opened his mouth and shut it again. With that kind he always had trouble with his impulses. He wanted to say, "You're goddam right you are." He did say, "I mean we're going to find that Santa Claus, and when we do we'll see. If we can't see him for it we'll have to look further, and we'll expect all of you to help us. I'm taking it for granted you'll all want to help. Don't you want to, Mrs. Jerome?"

"I would help if I could, but I know nothing about it. I only know that my very dear friend is dead, and I don't intend to be abused and threatened. What about the poison?"

"You know about it. You have been questioned about it."

"I know I have, but what about it?"

"It must have been apparent from the questions. The medical examiner thinks it was cyanide and expects the autopsy to verify it. Emil Hatch uses potassium cyanide in his work with metals and plating, and there is a large jar of it on a cupboard shelf in the workshop one floor below, and there is a stair from Bottweill's office to the workroom. Anyone who knew that, and who also knew that Bottweill kept a case of Pernod in a cabinet in his office, and an open bottle of it in a drawer of his desk, couldn't have asked for a better setup. Four of you have admitted knowing both of those things. Three of you—Mrs. Jerome, Leo Jerome, and Archie Goodwin—admit they knew about the Pernod but deny they knew about the potassium cyanide. That will—"

"That's not true! She did know about it!"

Mrs. Perry Porter Jerome's hand shot out across her son's knees and slapped Cherry Quon's cheek or mouth or both. Her son grabbed her arm. Alfred Kiernan sprang to his feet, and for a second I thought he was going to sock Mrs. Jerome, and he did too, and possibly he would have if Margot Dickey hadn't jerked at his coattail. Cherry put her hand to her face but, except for that, didn't move.

20

"Sit down," Stebbins told Kiernan. "Take it easy. Miss Quon, you say Mrs. Jerome knew about the potassium cyanide?"

"Of course she did." Cherry's chirp was pitched lower than normal, but it was still a chirp. "In the workshop one day I heard Mr. Hatch telling her how he used it and how careful he had to be."

"Mr. Hatch? Do you verify—"

"Nonsense," Mrs. Jerome snapped. "What if he did? Perhaps he did. I had forgotten all about it. I told you I won't tolerate this abuse!"

Purley eyed her. "Look here, Mrs. Jerome. When we find that Santa Claus, if it was someone who knew Bottweill and had a motive, that may settle it. If not, it won't help anyone to talk about abuse, and that includes you. So far as I know now, only one of you has told us a lie. You. That's on the record. I'm telling you, and all of you, lies only make it harder for you, but sometimes they make it easier for us. I'll leave it at that for now. Mr. Kiernan and Mr. Hatch, these men"—he aimed a thumb over his shoulder at two dicks standing back of him—"will take you downtown. The rest of you can go, but remember what I said. Goodwin, I want to see you."

He had already seen me, but I wouldn't make a point of it. Kiernan, however, had a point to make, and made it: he had to leave last so he could lock up. It was so arranged. The three women, Leo Jerome, and Stebbins and I took the elevator down, leaving the two dicks with Kiernan and Hatch. Down on the sidewalk, as they headed in different directions, I could see no sign of tails taking after them. It was still snowing, a fine prospect for Christmas and the street cleaners. There were two police cars at the curb, and Purley went to one and opened the door and motioned to me to get in.

I objected. "If I'm invited downtown too I'm willing to oblige, but I'm going to eat first. I damn near starved to death there once."

"You're not wanted downtown, not right now. Get in out of the snow."

I did so, and slid across under the wheel to make

21

room for him. He needs room. He joined me and pulled the door shut.

"If we're going to sit here," I suggested, "we might as well be rolling. Don't bother to cross town, just drop me at Thirty-fifth."

He objected. "I don't like to drive and talk. Or listen. What were you doing there today?"

"I've told you. Having fun. Three kinds of champagne. Miss Dickey invited me."

"I'm giving you another chance. You were the only outsider there. Why? You're nothing special to Miss Dickey. She was going to marry Bottweill. Why?"

"Ask her."

"We have asked her. She says there was no particular reason, she knew Bottweill liked you, and they've regarded you as one of them since you found some tapestries for them. She stuttered around about it. What I say, any time I find you anywhere near a murder, I want to know. I'm giving you another chance."

So she hadn't mentioned the marriage license. Good for her. I would rather have eaten all the snow that had fallen since noon than explain that damn license to Sergeant Stebbins or Inspector Cramer. That was why I had gone through the wastebasket. "Thanks for the chance," I told him, "but I can't use it. I've told you everything I saw and heard there today." That put me in a class with Mrs. Jerome, since I had left out my little talk with Margot. "I've told you all I know about those people. Lay off and go find your murderer."

"I know you, Goodwin."

"Yeah, you've even called me Archie. I treasure that memory."

"I know you." His head was turned on his bull neck, and our eyes were meeting. "Do you expect me to believe that guy got out of that room and away without you knowing it?"

"Nuts. I was kneeling on the floor, watching a man die, and they were around us. Anyway, you're just

22

talking to hear yourself. You don't think I was accessory to the murder or to the murderer's escape."

"I didn't say I did. Even if he was wearing gloves —and what for if not to leave no prints?—I don't say he was the murderer. But if you knew who he was and didn't want him involved in it, and let him get away, and if you let us wear out our ankles looking for him, what about that?"

"That would be bad. If I asked my advice I would be against it."

"Goddam it," he barked, "do you know who he is?"

"No."

"Did you or Wolfe have anything to do with getting him there?"

"No."

"All right, pile out. They'll be wanting you downtown."

"I hope not tonight. I'm tired." I opened the door. "You have my address." I stepped out into the snow, and he started the engine and rolled off.

It should have been a good hour for an empty taxi, but in a Christmas-season snowstorm it took me ten minutes to find one. When it pulled up in front of the old brownstone on West Thirty-fifth Street it was eight minutes to eight.

As usual in my absence, the chain-bolt was on, and I had to ring for Fritz to let me in. I asked him if Wolfe was back, and he said yes, he was at dinner. As I put my hat on the shelf and my coat on a hanger I asked if there was any left for me, and he said plenty, and moved aside for me to precede him down the hall to the door of the dining room. Fritz has fine manners.

Wolfe, in his oversized chair at the end of the table, told me good evening, not snapping or barking. I returned it, got seated at my place, picked up my napkin, and apologized for being late. Fritz came, from the kitchen, with a warm plate, a platter of braised boned ducklings, and a dish of potatoes baked with mushrooms and cheese. I took enough. Wolfe asked if it was still snowing and I said yes. After a good mouthful had been disposed of, I spoke.

23

"As you know, I approve of your rule not to discuss business during a meal, but I've got something on my chest and it's not business. It's personal."

He grunted. "The death of Mr. Bottweill was reported on the radio at seven o'clock. You were there."

"Yeah. I was there. I was kneeling by him while he died." I replenished my mouth. Damn the radio. I hadn't intended to mention the murder until I had dealt with the main issue from my standpoint. When there was room enough for my tongue to work I went on, "I'll report on that in full if you want it, but I doubt if there's a job in it. Mrs. Perry Porter Jerome is the only suspect with enough jack to pay your fee, and she has already notified Purley Stebbins that she won't be abused. Besides, when they find Santa Claus that may settle it. What I want to report on happened before Bottweill died. That marriage license I showed you is for the birds. Miss Dickey has called it off. I am out two bucks. She told me she had decided to marry Bottweill."

He was sopping a crust in the sauce on his plate. "Indeed," he said.

"Yes, sir. It was a jolt, but I would have recovered, in time. Then ten minutes later Bottweill was dead. Where does that leave me? Sitting around up there through the routine, I considered it. Perhaps I could get her back now, but no thank you. That license has been destroyed. I get another one, another two bucks, and then she tells me she has decided to marry Joe Doakes. I'm going to forget her. I'm going to blot her out."

I resumed on the duckling. Wolfe was busy chewing. When he could he said, "For me, of course, this is satisfactory."

"I know it is. Do you want to hear about Bottweill?"

"After dinner."

"Okay. How did you make out with Thompson?"

But that didn't appeal to him as a dinner topic either. In fact, nothing did. Usually he likes table talk, about anything from refrigerators to Republicans, but apparently the trip to Long Island and back, with all

24

its dangers, had tired him out. It suited me all right, since I had had a noisy afternoon too and could stand a little silence. When we had both done well with the duckling and potatoes and salad and baked pears and cheese and coffee, he pushed back his chair.

"There's a book," he said, "that I want to look at. It's up in your room—*Here and Now*, by Herbert Block. Will you bring it down, please?"

Though it meant climbing two flights with a full stomach, I was glad to oblige, out of appreciation for his calm acceptance of my announcement of my shattered hopes. He could have been very vocal. So I mounted the stairs cheerfully, went to my room, and crossed to the shelves where I keep a few books. There were only a couple of dozen of them, and I knew where each one was, but *Here and Now* wasn't there. Where it should have been was a gap. I looked around, saw a book on the dresser, and stepped to it. It was *Here and Now*, and lying on top of it was a pair of white cotton gloves.

I gawked.

IV

I would like to say that I caught on immediately, the second I spotted them, but I didn't. I had picked them up and looked them over, and put one of them on and taken it off again, before I fully realized that there was only one possible explanation. Having realized it, instantly there was a traffic jam inside my skull, horns blowing, brakes squealing, head-on collisions. To deal with it I went to a chair and sat. It took me maybe a minute to reach my first clear conclusion.

He had taken this method of telling me he was Santa Claus, instead of just telling me, because he wanted me to think it over on my own before we talked it over together.

Why did he want me to think it over on my own? That took a little longer, but with the traffic under control I found my way through to the only acceptable answer. He had decided to give up his trip to see Thompson, and instead to arrange with Bottweill to attend the Christmas party disguised as Santa Claus, because the idea of a woman living in his house—or of the only alternative, my leaving—had made him absolutely desperate, and he had to see for himself. He had to see Margot and me together, and to talk with her if possible. If he found out that the marriage license was a hoax he would have me by the tail; he could tell me he would be delighted to welcome my bride and watch me wriggle out. If he found that I really meant it he would know what he was up against and go on from there. The point was this, that he had shown what he really thought of me. He had shown that rather than lose me he would do something that

26

he wouldn't have done for any fee anybody could name. He would rather have gone without beer for a week than admit it, but now he was a fugitive from justice in a murder case and needed me. So he had to let me know, but he wanted it understood that that aspect of the matter was not to be mentioned. The assumption would be that he had gone to Bottweill's instead of Long Island because he loved to dress up like Santa Claus and tend bar.

A cell in my brain tried to get the right of way for the question, considering this development, how big a raise should I get after New Year's? but I waved it to the curb.

I thought over other aspects. He had worn the gloves so I couldn't recognize his hands. Where did he get them? What time had he got to Bottweill's and who had seen him? Did Fritz know where he was going? How had he got back home? But after a little of that I realized that he hadn't sent me up to my room to ask myself questions he could answer, so I went back to considering whether there was anything else he wanted me to think over alone. Deciding there wasn't, after chewing it thoroughly, I got *Here and Now* and the gloves from the dresser, went to the stairs and descended, and entered the office.

From behind his desk, he glared at me as I crossed over.

"Here it is," I said, and handed him the book. "And much obliged for the gloves." I held them up, one in each hand, dangling them from thumb and fingertip.

"It is no occasion for clowning," he growled.

"It sure isn't." I dropped the gloves on my desk, whirled my chair, and sat. "Where do we start? Do you want to know what happened after you left?"

"The details can wait. First where we stand. Was Mr. Cramer there?"

"Yes. Certainly."

"Did he get anywhere?"

"No. He probably won't until he finds Santa Claus. Until they find Santa Claus they won't dig very hard at the others. The longer it takes to find him the surer they'll be he's it. Three things about him: no-body knows who he was, he beat it, and he wore gloves. A thousand men are looking for him. You were right to wear the gloves, I would have recognized your hands, but where did you get them?"

"At a store on Ninth Avenue. Confound it, I didn't know a man was going to be murdered!"

"I know you didn't. May I ask some questions?"

He scowled. I took it for yes. "When did you phone Bottweill to arrange it?"

"At two-thirty yesterday afternoon. You had gone to the bank."

"Have you any reason to think he told anyone about it?"

"No. He said he wouldn't."

"I know he got the costume, so that's okay. When you left here today at twelve-thirty did you go straight to Bottweill's?"

"No. I left at that hour because you and Fritz expected me to. I stopped to buy the gloves, and met him at Rusterman's, and we had lunch. From there we took a cab to his place, arriving shortly after two o'clock, and took his private elevator up to his office. Immediately upon entering his office, he got a bottle of Pernod from a drawer of his desk, said he always had a little after lunch, and invited me to join him. I declined. He poured a liberal portion in a glass, about two ounces, drank it in two gulps, and returned the bottle to the drawer."

"My God." I whistled. "The cops would like to know *that*."

"No doubt. The costume was there in a box. There is a dressing room at the rear of his office, with a bathroom—"

"I know. I've used it."

"I took the costume there and put it on. He had ordered the largest size, but it was a squeeze and it took a while. I was in there half an hour or more. When I re-entered the office it was empty, but soon Bottweill came, up the stairs from the workshop, and helped me with the mask and wig. They had barely been adjusted when Emil Hatch and Mrs. Jerome and her son appeared, also coming up the stairs from the workshop. I left, going to the studio, and found Miss Quon and Miss Dickey and Mr. Kiernan there."

"And before long I was there. Then no one saw you unmasked. When did you put the gloves on?"

"The last thing. Just before I entered the studio."

"Then you may have left prints. I know, you didn't know there was going to be a murder. You left your clothes in the dressing room? Are you sure you got everything when you left?"

"Yes. I am not a complete ass."

I let that by. "Why didn't you leave the gloves in the elevator with the costume?"

"Because they hadn't come with it, and I thought it better to take them."

"That private elevator is at the rear of the hall downstairs. Did anyone see you leaving it or passing through the hall?"

"No. The hall was empty."

"How did you get home? Taxi?"

"No. Fritz didn't expect me until six or later. I walked to the public library, spent some two hours there, and then took a cab."

I pursed my lips and shook my head to indicate sympathy. That was his longest and hardest tramp since Montenegro. Over a mile. Fighting his way through the blizzard, in terror of the law on his tail. But all the return I got for my look of sympathy was a scowl, so I let loose. I laughed. I put my head back and let it come. I had wanted to ever since I had learned he was Santa Claus, but had been too busy thinking. It was bottled up in me, and I let it out, good. I was about to taper off to a cackle when he exploded.

"Confound it," he bellowed, "marry and be damned!"

That was dangerous. That attitude could easily get us onto the aspect he had sent me up to my room to think over alone, and if we got started on that anything could happen. It called for tact.

"I beg your pardon," I said. "Something caught in my throat. Do you want to describe the situation, or do you want me to?"

"I would like to hear you try," he said grimly.

"Yes, sir. I suspect that the only thing to do is to phone Inspector Cramer right now and invite him to come and have a chat, and when he comes open the bag. That will—"

"No. I will not do that."

"Then, next best, I go to him and spill it there. Of course—"

"No." He meant every word of it.

"Okay, I'll describe it. They'll mark time on the others until they find Santa Claus. They've got to find him. If he left any prints they'll compare them with every file they've got, and sooner or later they'll get to yours. They'll cover all the stores for sales of white cotton gloves to men. They'll trace Bottweill's movements and learn that he lunched with you at Rusterman's, and you left together, and they'll trace you to Bottweill's place. Of course your going there won't prove you were Santa Claus, you might talk your way out of that, and it will account for your prints if they find some, but what about the gloves? They'll trace that sale if you give them time, and with a description of the buyer they'll find Santa Claus. You're sunk."

I had never seen his face blacker.

"If you sit tight till they find him," I argued, "it will be quite a nuisance. Cramer has been itching for years to lock you up, and any judge would commit you as a material witness who had run out. Whereas if you call Cramer now, and I mean now, and invite him to come and have some beer, while it will still be a nuisance, it will be bearable. Of course he'll want to know why you went there and played Santa Claus, but you can tell him anything you please. Tell him you bet me a hundred bucks, or what the hell, make it a grand, that you could be in a room with me for ten minutes and I wouldn't recognize you. I'll be glad to cooperate."

I leaned forward. "Another thing. If you wait till they find you, you won't dare tell them that Bottweill took a drink from that bottle shortly after two o'clock and it didn't hurt him. If you told about that after they dug you up, they could book you for withholding evidence, and they probably would, and make it stick. If you get Cramer here now and tell him he'll appreciate it, though naturally he won't say so. He's probably at his office. Shall I ring him?"

"No. I will not confess that performance to Mr. Cramer. I will not unfold the morning paper to a disclosure of that outlandish masquerade."

"Then you're going to sit and read *Here and Now* until they come with a warrant?"

"No. That would be fatuous." He took in air through his mouth, as far down as it would go, and let it out through his nose. "I'm going to find the murderer and present him to Mr. Cramer. There's nothing else."

"Oh. You are."

"Yes."

"You might have said so and saved my breath, instead of letting me spout."

"I wanted to see if your appraisal of the situation agreed with mine. It does."

"That's fine. Then you also know that we may have two weeks and we may have two minutes. At this very second some expert may be phoning Homicide to say that he has found fingerprints that match on the card of Wolfe, Nero—"

The phone rang, and I jerked around as if someone had stuck a needle in me. Maybe we wouldn't have even two minutes. My hand wasn't trembling as I lifted the receiver, I hope. Wolfe seldom lifts his until I have found out who it is, but that time he did.

"Nero Wolfe's office, Archie Goodwin speaking."

"This is the District Attorney's office, Mr. Goodwin. Regarding the murder of Kurt Bottweill. We would like you to be here at ten o'clock tomorrow morning."

"All right. Sure."

"At ten o'clock sharp, please."

"I'll be there."

31

We hung up. Wolfe sighed. I sighed.

"Well," I said, "I've already told them six times that I know absolutely nothing about Santa Claus, so they may not ask me again. If they do, it will be interesting to compare my voice when I'm lying with when I'm telling the truth."

He grunted. "Now. I want a complete report of what happened there after I left, but first I want background. In your intimate association with Miss Dickey you must have learned things about those people. What?"

"Not much." I cleared my throat. "I guess I'll have to explain something. My association with Miss Dickey was not intimate." I stopped. It wasn't easy.

"Choose your own adjective. I meant no innuendo."

"It's not a question of adjectives. Miss Dickey is a good dancer, exceptionally good, and for the past couple of months I have been taking her here and there, some six or eight times altogether. Monday evening at the Flamingo Club she asked me to do her a favor. She said Bottweill was giving her a runaround, that he had been going to marry her for a year but kept stalling, and she wanted to do something. She said Cherry Quon was making a play for him, and she didn't intend to let Cherry take the rail. She asked me to get a marriage-license blank and fill it out for her and me and give it to her. She would show it to Bottweill and tell him now or never. It struck me as a good deed with no risk involved, and, as I say, she is a good dancer. Tuesday afternoon I got a blank, no matter how, and that evening, up in my room, I filled it in, including a fancy signature."

Wolfe made a noise.

"That's all," I said, "except that I want to make it clear that I had no intention of showing it to you. I did that on the spur of the moment when you picked up your book. Your memory is as good as mine. Also, to close it up, no doubt you noticed that today just before Bottweill and Mrs. Jerome joined the party Margot and I stepped aside for a little chat. She told me the license did the trick. Her words were, 'Perfect, simply perfect.' She said that last evening, in his office, he tore the license up and put the pieces in his wastebasket. That's okay, the cops didn't find them. I looked before they came, and the pieces weren't there."

His mouth was working, but he didn't open it. He didn't dare. He would have liked to tear into me, to tell me that my insufferable flummery had got him into this awful mess, but if he did so he would be dragging in the aspect he didn't want mentioned. He saw that in time, and saw that I saw it. His mouth worked, but that was all. Finally he spoke.

"Then you are not on intimate terms with Miss Dickey."

"No, sir."

"Even so, she must have spoken of that establishment and those people." ·

"Some, yes."

"And one of them killed Bottweill. The poison was put in the bottle between two-ten, when I saw him take a drink, and three-thirty when Kiernan went and got the bottle. No one came up in the private elevator during the half-hour or more I was in the dressing room. I was getting into that costume and gave no heed to footsteps or other sounds in the office, but the elevator shaft adjoins the dressing room, and I would have heard it. It is a strong probability that the opportunity was even narrower, that the poison was put in the bottle while I was in the dressing room, since three of them were in the office with Bottweill when I left. It must be assumed that one of those three, or one of the three in the studio, had grasped an earlier opportunity. What about them?"

"Not much. Mostly from Monday evening, when Margot was talking about Bottweill. So it's all hearsay, from her. Mrs. Jerome has put half a million in the business—probably you should divide that by two at least—and thinks she owns him. Or thought. She was jealous of Margot and Cherry. As for Leo, if his mother was dishing out the dough he expected to inherit to a guy who was trying to corner the world's supply of gold leaf, and possibly might also marry him, and if he knew about the jar of poison in the workshop, he might have been tempted. Kiernan, I don't know, but from a remark Margot made and from the way he looked at Cherry this afternoon, I suspect he would like to mix some Irish with her Chinese and Indian and Dutch, and if he thought Bottweill had him stymied he might have been tempted too. So much for hearsay."

"Mr. Hatch?"

"Nothing on him from Margot, but dealing with him during the tapestry job, I wouldn't have been surprised if he had wiped out the whole bunch on general principles. His heart pumps acid instead of blood. He's a creative artist, he told me so. He practically told me that he was responsible for the success of that enterprise but got no credit. He didn't tell me that he regarded Bottweill as a phony and a fourflusher, but he did. You may remember that I told you he had a persecution complex and you told me to stop using other people's jargon."

"That's four of them. Miss Dickey?"

I raised my brows. "I got her a license to marry, not to kill. If she was lying when she said it worked, she's almost as good a liar as she is a dancer. Maybe she is. If it didn't work she might have been tempted too."

"And Miss Quon?"

"She's half Oriental. I'm not up on Orientals, but I understood they slant their eyes to keep you guessing. That's what makes them inscrutable. If I had to be poisoned by one of that bunch I would want it to be her. Except for what Margot told me—"

The doorbell rang. That was worse than the phone. If they had hit on Santa Claus's trail and it led to Nero Wolfe, Cramer was much more apt to come than to call. Wolfe and I exchanged glances. Looking at my wristwatch and seeing 10:08, I arose, went to the hall and flipped the switch for the stoop light, and took a look through the one-way glass panel of the front door. I have good eyes, but the figure was muffled in a heavy coat with a hood, so I stepped halfway to the door to make sure. Then I returned to the office and told Wolfe, "Cherry Quon. Alone."

He frowned. "I wanted—" He cut it off. "Very well. Bring her in."

V

As I have said, Cherry was highly decorative, and she went fine with the red leather chair at the end of Wolfe's desk. It would have held three of her. She had let me take her coat in the hall and still had on the neat little woolen number she had worn at the party. It wasn't exactly yellow, but there was yellow in it. I would have called if off-gold, and it and the red chair and the tea tint of her smooth little carved face would have made a very nice kodachrome.

She sat on the edge, her spine straight and her hands together in her lap. "I was afraid to telephone," she said, "because you might tell me not to come. So I just came. Will you forgive me?"

Wolfe grunted. No commitment. She smiled at him, a friendly smile, or so I thought. After all, she was half Oriental.

"I must get myself together," she chirped. "I'm nervous because it's so exciting to be here." She turned her head. "There's the globe, and the bookshelves, and the safe, and the couch, and of course Archie Goodwin. And you. You behind your desk in your enormous chair! Oh, I know this place! I have read about you so much—everything there is, I think. It's exciting to be here, actually here in this chair, and see you. Of course I saw you this afternoon, but that wasn't the same thing, you could have been anybody in that silly Santa Claus costume. I wanted to pull your whiskers."

She laughed, a friendly little tinkle like a bell.

I think I looked bewildered. That was my idea, after it had got through my ears to the switchboard inside and been routed. I was too busy handling my face to look at Wolfe, but he was probably even busier, since she was looking straight at him. I moved my eyes to him when he spoke.

"If I understand you, Miss Quon, I'm at a loss. If you think you saw me this afternoon in a Santa Claus costume, you're mistaken."

"Oh, I'm sorry!" she exclaimed. "Then you haven't told them?"

"My dear madam." His voice sharpened. "If you must talk in riddles, talk to Mr. Goodwin. He enjoys them."

"But I *am* sorry, Mr. Wolfe. I should have explained first how I know. This morning at breakfast Kurt told me you had phoned him and arranged to appear at the party as Santa Claus, and this afternoon I asked him if you had come and he said you had and you were putting on the costume. That's how I know. But you haven't told the police? Then it's a good thing I haven't told them either, isn't it?"

"This is interesting," Wolfe said coldly. "What do you expect to accomplish by this fantastic folderol?"

She shook her pretty little head. "You, with so much sense. You must see that it's no use. If I tell them, even if they don't like to believe me they will investigate. I know they can't investigate as well as you can, but surely they will find something."

He shut his eyes, tightened his lips, and leaned back in his chair. I kept mine open, on her. She weighed about a hundred and two. I could carry her under one arm with my other hand clamped on her mouth. Putting her in the spare room upstairs wouldn't do, since she could open a window and scream, but there was a cubbyhole in the basement, next to Fritz's room, with an old couch in it. Or, as an alternative, I could get a gun from my desk drawer and shoot her. Probably no one knew she had come here.

Wolfe opened his eyes and straightened up. "Very well. It is still fantastic, but I concede that you could create an unpleasant situation by taking that yarn to the police. I don't suppose you came here merely to tell me that you intend to. What do you intend?"

"I think we understand each other," she chirped.

"I understand only that you want something. What?"

"You are so direct," she complained. "So very abrupt, that I must have said something wrong. But I do want something. You see, since the police think it was the man who acted Santa Claus and ran away, they may not get on the right track until it's too late. You wouldn't want that, would you?"

No reply.

"I wouldn't want it," she said, and her hands on her lap curled into little fists. "I wouldn't want whoever killed Kurt to get away, no matter who it was, but you see, I know who killed him. I have told the police, but they won't listen until they find Santa Claus, or if they listen they think I'm just a jealous cat, and besides, I'm an Oriental and their ideas of Orientals are very primitive. I was going to make them listen by telling them who Santa Claus was, but I know how they feel about you from what I've read, and I was afraid they would try to prove it was you who killed Kurt, and of course it could have been you, and you did run away, and they still wouldn't listen to me when I told them who did kill him."

She stopped for breath. Wolfe inquired, "Who did?"

She nodded. "I'll tell you. Margot Dickey and Kurt were having an affair. A few months ago Kurt began on me, and it was hard for me because I—I—" She frowned for a word, and found one. "I had a feeling for him. I had a strong feeling. But you see, I am a virgin, and I wouldn't give in to him. I don't know what I would have done if I hadn't known he was having an affair with Margot, but I did know, and I told him the first man I slept with would be my husband. He said he was willing to give up Margot, but even if he did he couldn't marry me on account of Mrs. Jerome, because she would stop backing him with her

38

money. I don't know what he was to Mrs. Jerome, but I know what she was to him."

Her hands opened and closed again to be fists. "That went on and on, but Kurt had a feeling for me too. Last night late, it was after midnight, he phoned me that he had broken with Margot for good and he wanted to marry me. He wanted to come and see me, but I told him I was in bed and we would see each other in the morning. He said that would be at the studio with other people there, so finally I said I would go to his apartment for breakfast, and I did, this morning. But I am still a virgin, Mr. Wolfe."

He was focused on her with half-closed eyes. "That is your privilege, madam."

"Oh," she said. "Is it a privilege? It was there, at breakfast, that he told me about you, your arranging to be Santa Claus. When I got to the studio I was surprised to see Margot there, and how friendly she was. That was part of her plan, to be friendly and cheerful with everyone. She has told the police that Kurt was going to marry her, that they decided last night to get married next week. Christmas week. I am a Christian."

Wolfe stirred in his chair. "Have we reached the point? Did Miss Dickey kill Mr. Bottweill?"

"Yes. Of course she did."

"Have you told the police that?"

"Yes. I didn't tell them all I have told you, but enough."

"With evidence?"

"No. I have no evidence."

"Then you're vulnerable to an action for slander."

She opened her fists and turned her palms up. "Does that matter? When I know I'm right? When I *know* it? But she was so clever, the way she did it, that there can't be any evidence. Everybody there today knew about the poison, and they all had a chance to put it in the bottle. They can never prove she did it. They can't even prove she is lying when she says Kurt was going to marry her, because he is dead. She acted today the way she would have acted if that had been

39

true. But it has got to be proved somehow. There has got to be evidence to prove it."

"And you want me to get it?"

She let that pass. "What I was thinking, Mr. Wolfe, you are vulnerable too. There will always be the danger that the police will find out who Santa Claus was, and if they find it was you and you didn't tell them—"

"I haven't conceded that," Wolfe snapped.

"Then we'll just say there will always be the danger that I'll tell them what Kurt told me, and you did concede that that would be unpleasant. So it would be better if the evidence proved who killed Kurt and also proved who Santa Claus was. Wouldn't it?"

"Go on."

"So I thought how easy it would be for you to get the evidence. You have men who do things for you, who would do anything for you, and one of them can say that you asked him to go there and be Santa Claus, and he did. Of course it couldn't be Mr. Goodwin, since he was at the party, and it would have to be a man they couldn't prove was somewhere else. He can say that while he was in the dressing room putting on the costume he heard someone in the office and peeked out to see who it was, and he saw Margot Dickey get the bottle from the desk drawer and put something in it and put the bottle back in the drawer, and go out. That must have been when she did it, because Kurt always took a drink of Pernod when he came back from lunch."

Wolfe was rubbing his lip with a fingertip. "I see," he muttered.

She wasn't through. "He can say," she went on, "that he ran away because he was frightened and wanted to tell you about it first. I don't think they would do anything to him if he went to them tomorrow morning and told them all about it, would they? Just like me. I don't think they would do anything to me if I went to them tomorrow morning and told them I had remembered that Kurt told me that you were going to be Santa Claus, and this afternoon he told me you were in the dressing room putting on the costume. That would be the same kind of thing, wouldn't it?"

40

Her little carved mouth thinned and widened with a smile. "That's what I want," she chirped. "Did I say it so you understand it?"

"You did indeed," Wolfe assured her. "You put it admirably."

"Would it be better, instead of him going to tell them, for you to have Inspector Cramer come here, and you tell him? You could have the man here. You see, I know how you do things, from all I have read."

"That might be better," he allowed. His tone was dry but not hostile. I could see a muscle twitching beneath his right ear, but she couldn't. "I suppose, Miss Quon, it is futile to advance the possibility that one of the others killed him, and if so it would be a pity—"

"Excuse me. I interrupt." The chirp was still a chirp, but it had hard steel in it. "I know she killed him."

"I don't. And even if I bow to your conviction, before I could undertake the stratagem you propose I would have to make sure there are no facts that would scuttle it. It won't take me long. You'll hear from me tomorrow. I'll want—"

She interrupted again. "I can't wait longer than tomorrow morning to tell them what Kurt told me."

"Pfui. You can and will. The moment you disclose that, you no longer have a whip to dangle at me. You will hear from me tomorrow. Now I want to think. Archie?"

I left my chair. She looked up at me and back at Wolfe. For some seconds she sat, considering, inscrutable of course, then stood up.

"It was very exciting to be here," she said, the steel gone, "to see you here. You must forgive me for not phoning. I hope it will be early tomorrow." She turned and headed for the door, and I followed.

After I had helped her on with her hooded coat, and let her out, and watched her picking her way down the seven steps, I shut the door, put the chain-bolt on, returned to the office, and told Wolfe, "It has stopped snowing. Who do you think will be best for it, Saul or Fred or Orrie or Bill?"

"Sit down," he growled. "You see through women. Well?"

"Not that one. I pass. I wouldn't bet a dime on her one way or the other. Would you?"

"No. She is probably a liar and possibly a murderer. Sit down. I must have everything that happened there today after I left. Every word and gesture."

I sat and gave it to him. Including the question period, it took an hour and thirty-five minutes. It was after one o'clock when he pushed his chair back, levered his bulk upright, told me good night, and went up to bed.

VI

At half past two the following afternoon, Saturday, I sat in a room in a building on Leonard Street, the room where I had once swiped an assistant district attorney's lunch. There would be no need for me to repeat the performance, since I had just come back from Ost's restaurant, where I had put away a plateful of pig's knuckles and sauerkraut.

As far as I knew, there had not only been no steps to frame Margot for murder; there had been no steps at all. Since Wolfe is up in the plant rooms every morning from nine to eleven, and since he breakfasts from a tray up in his room, and since I was expected downtown at ten o'clock, I had buzzed him on the house phone a little before nine to ask for instructions and had been told that he had none. Downtown Assistant DA Farrell, after letting me wait in the anteroom for an hour, had spent two hours with me, together with a stenographer and a dick who had been on the scene Friday afternoon, going back and forth and zigzag, not only over what I had already reported, but also over my previous association with the Bottweill personnel. He only asked me once if I knew anything about Santa Claus, so I only had to lie once, if you don't count my omitting any mention of the marriage license. When he called a recess and told me to come back at two-thirty, on my way to Ost's for the pig's knuckles I phoned Wolfe to tell him I didn't know when I would be home, and again he had no instructions. I said I doubted if Cherry Quon would wait until after New Year's to spill the beans, and he said he did too and hung up.

43

When I was ushered back into Farrell's office at two-thirty he was alone—no stenographer and no dick. He asked me if I had had a good lunch, and even waited for me to answer, handed me some type-written sheets, and leaned back in his chair.

"Read it over," he said, "and see if you want to sign it."

His tone seemed to imply that I might not, so I went over it carefully, five full pages. Finding no editorial revisions to object to, I pulled my chair forward to a corner of his desk, put the statement on the desk top, and got my pen from my pocket.

"Wait a minute," Farrell said. "You're not a bad guy even if you are cocky, and why not give you a break? That says specifically that you have reported everything you did there yesterday afternoon."

"Yeah, I've read it. So?"

"So who put your fingerprints on some of the pieces of paper in Bottweill's wastebasket?"

"I'll be damned," I said. "I forgot to put gloves on."

"All right, you're cocky. I already know that." His eyes were pinning me. "You must have gone through that wastebasket, every item, when you went to Bottweill's office ostensibly to look for Santa Claus, and you hadn't just forgotten it. You don't forget things. So you have deliberately left it out. I want to know why, and I want to know what you took from that wastebasket and what you did with it."

I grinned at him. "I am also damned because I thought I knew how thorough they are and apparently I didn't. I wouldn't have supposed they went so far as to dust the contents of a wastebasket when there was nothing to connect them, but I see I was wrong, and I hate to be wrong." I shrugged. "Well, we learn something new every day." I screwed the statement around to position, signed it at the bottom of the last page, slid it across to him, and folded the carbon copy and put it in my pocket.

"I'll write it in if you insist," I told him, "but I doubt if it's worth the trouble. Santa Claus had run, Kiernan was calling the police, and I guess I was a little rattled. I must have looked around for something that might give me a line on Santa Claus, and my eye lit on the wastebasket, and I went through it. I haven't mentioned it because it wasn't very bright, and I like people to think I'm bright, especially cops. There's your why. As for what I took, the answer is nothing. I dumped the wastebasket, put everything back in, and took nothing. Do you want me to write that in?"

"No. I want to discuss it. I know you *are* bright. And you weren't rattled. You don't rattle. I want to know the real reason you went through the wastebasket, what you were after, whether you got it, and what you did with it."

It cost me more than an hour, twenty minutes of which were spent in the office of the District Attorney himself, with Farrell and another assistant present. At one point it looked as if they were going to hold me as a material witness, but that takes a warrant, the Christmas weekend had started, and there was nothing to show that I had monkeyed with anything that could be evidence, so finally they shooed me out, after I had handwritten an insert in my statement. It was too bad keeping such important public servants sitting there while I copied the insert on my carbon, but I like to do things right.

By the time I got home it was ten minutes past four, and of course Wolfe wasn't in the office, since his afternoon session up in the plant rooms is from four to six. There was no note on my desk from him, so apparently there were still no instructions, but there was information on it. My desk ashtray, which is mostly for decoration since I seldom smoke—a gift, not to Wolfe but to me, from a former client—is a jade bowl six inches across. It was there in its place, and in it were three stubs from Pharaoh cigarettes.

Saul Panzer smokes Pharaohs, Egyptians. I suppose a few other people do too, but the chance that one of them had been sitting at my desk while I was gone was too slim to bother with. And not only had Saul been there, but Wolfe wanted me to know it, since one of the eight million things he will not tolerate in the office is ashtrays with remains. He will actually walk clear to the bathroom himself to empty one.

So steps were being taken, after all. What steps? Saul, a free lance and the best operative anywhere around, asks and gets sixty bucks a day, and is worth twice that. Wolfe had not called him in for any routine errand, and of course the idea that he had undertaken to sell him on doubling for Santa Claus never entered my head. Framing someone for murder, even a woman who might be guilty, was not in his bag of tricks. I got at the house phone and buzzed the plant rooms, and after a wait had Wolfe's voice in my ear.

"Yes, Fritz?"

"Not Fritz. Me. I'm back. Nothing urgent to report. They found my prints on stuff in the wastebasket, but I escaped without loss of blood. Is it all right for me to empty my ashtray?"

"Yes. Please do so."

"Then what do I do?"

"I'll tell you at six o'clock. Possibly earlier."

He hung up. I went to the safe and looked in the cash drawer to see if Saul had been supplied with generous funds, but the cash was as I had last seen it and there was no entry in the book. I emptied the ashtray. I went to the kitchen, where I found Fritz pouring a mixture into a bowl of fresh pork tenderloin, and said I hoped Saul had enjoyed his lunch, and Fritz said he hadn't stayed for lunch. So steps must have been begun right after I left in the morning. I went back to the office, read over the carbon copy of my statement before filing it, and passed the time by thinking up eight different steps that Saul might have been assigned, but none of them struck me as promising. A little after five the phone rang and I answered. It was Saul. He said he was glad to know I was back home safe, and I said I was too.

"Just a message for Mr. Wolfe," he said. "Tell him everything is set, no snags."

"That's all?"

"Right. I'll be seeing you."

I cradled the receiver, sat a moment to consider whether to go up to the plant rooms or use the house phone, decided the latter would do, and pulled it to me and pushed the button. When Wolfe's voice came it was peevish; he hates to be disturbed up there.

"Yes?"

"Saul called and said to tell you everything is set, no snags. Congratulations. Am I in the way?"

"Oddly enough, no. Have chairs in place for visitors; ten should be enough. Four or five will come shortly after six o'clock; I hope not more. Others will come later."

"Refreshments?"

"Liquids, of course. Nothing else."

"Anything else for me?"

"No."

He was gone. Before going to the front room for chairs, and to the kitchen for supplies, I took time out to ask myself whether I had the slightest notion what kind of charade he was cooking up this time. I hadn't.

VII

It was four. They all arrived between six-fifteen and six-twenty—first Mrs. Perry Porter Jerome and her son Leo, then Cherry Quon, and last Emil Hatch. Mrs. Jerome copped the red leather chair, but I moved her, mink and all, to one of the yellow ones when Cherry came. I was willing to concede that Cherry might be headed for a very different kind of chair, wired for power, but even so I thought she rated that background and Mrs. Jerome didn't. By six-thirty, when I left them to cross the hall to the dining room, not a word had passed among them.

In the dining room Wolfe had just finished a bottle of beer. "Okay," I told him, "it's six-thirty-one. Only four. Kiernan and Margot Dickey haven't shown."

"Satisfactory." He arose. "Have they demanded information?"

"Two of them have, Hatch and Mrs. Jerome. I told them it will come from you, as instructed. That was easy, since I have none."

He headed for the office, and I followed. Though they didn't know, except Cherry, that he had poured champagne for them the day before, introductions weren't necessary because they had all met him during the tapestry hunt. After circling around Cherry in the red leather chair, he stood behind his desk to ask them how they did, then sat.

"I don't thank you for coming," he said, "because you came in your own interest, not mine. I sent—"

"I came," Hatch cut in, sourer than ever, "to find out what you're up to."

"You will," Wolfe assured him. "I sent each of you

48

an identical message, saying that Mr. Goodwin has certain information which he feels he must give the police not later than tonight, but I have persuaded him to let me discuss it with you first. Before I—"

"I didn't know others would be here," Mrs. Jerome blurted, glaring at Cherry.

"Neither did I," Hatch said, glaring at Mrs. Jerome.

Wolfe ignored it. "The message I sent Miss Quon was somewhat different, but that need not concern you. Before I tell you what Mr. Goodwin's information is, I need a few facts from you. For instance, I understand that any of you—including Miss Dickey and Mr. Kiernan, who will probably join us later—could have found an opportunity to put the poison in the bottle. Do any of you challenge that?"

Cherry, Mrs. Jerome, and Leo all spoke at once. Hatch merely looked sour.

Wolfe showed them a palm. "If you please. I point no finger of accusation at any of you. I merely say that none of you, including Miss Dickey and Mr. Kiernan, can prove that you had no opportunity. Can you?"

"Nuts." Leo Jerome was disgusted. "It was that guy playing Santa Claus. Of course it was. I was with Bottweill and my mother all the time, first in the workshop and then in his office. I can prove *that.*"

"But Bottweill is dead," Wolfe reminded him, "and your mother is your mother. Did you go up to the office a little before them, or did your mother go up a little before you and Bottweill did? Is there acceptable proof that you didn't? The others have the same problem. Miss Quon?"

There was no danger of Cherry's spoiling it. Wolfe had told me what he had told her on the phone: that he had made a plan which he thought she would find satisfactory, and if she came at a quarter past six she would see it work. She had kept her eyes fixed on him ever since he entered. Now she chirped, "If you mean I can't prove I wasn't in the office alone yesterday, no, I can't."

"Mr. Hatch?"

"I didn't come here to prove anything. I told you what I came for. What information has Goodwin got?"

"We'll get to that. A few more facts first. Mrs. Jerome, when did you learn that Bottweill had decided to marry Miss Quon?"

Leo shouted, "No!" but his mother was too busy staring at Wolfe to hear him. "What?" she croaked. Then she found her voice. "Kurt marry *her?* That little strumpet?"

Cherry didn't move a muscle, her eyes still on Wolfe.

"This is wonderful!" Leo said. "This is marvelous!"

"Not so damn wonderful," Emil Hatch declared. "I get the idea, Wolfe. Goodwin hasn't got any information, and neither have you. Why you wanted to get us together and start us clawing at each other, I don't see that, I don't know why you're interested, but maybe I'll find out if I give you a hand. This crowd has produced as fine a collection of venom as you could find. Maybe we all put poison in the bottle and that's why it was such a big dose. If it's true that Kurt had decided to marry Cherry, and Al Kiernan knew it, that would have done it. Al would have killed a hundred Kurts if it would get him Cherry. If Mrs. Jerome knew it, I would think she would have gone for Cherry instead of Kurt, but maybe she figured there would soon be another one and she might as well settle it for good. As for Leo, I think he rather liked Kurt, but what can you expect? Kurt was milking mamma of the pile Leo hoped to get some day, and I suspect that the pile is not all it's supposed to be. Actually—"

He stopped, and I left my chair. Leo was on his way up, obviously with the intention of plugging the creative artist. I moved to head him off, and at the same instant I gave him a shove and his mother jerked at his coattail. That not only halted him but nearly upset him, and with my other hand I steered him back onto his chair and then stood beside him.

Hatch inquired, "Shall I go on?"

"By all means," Wolfe said.

"Actually, though, Cherry would seem to be the most likely. She has the best brain of the lot and by far the strongest will. But I understand that while she says Kurt was going to marry her, Margot claims that he was going to marry *her*. Of course that complicates it, and anyway Margot would be my second choice. Margot has more than her share of the kind of pride that is only skin deep and therefore can't stand a scratch. If Kurt did decide to marry Cherry and told Margot so, he was even a bigger imbecile than I thought he was. Which brings us to me. I am in a class by myself. I despise all of them. If I had decided to take to poison I would have put it in the champagne as well as the Pernod, and I would have drunk vodka, which I prefer—and by the way, on that table is a bottle with the Korbeloff vodka label. I haven't had a taste of Korbeloff for fifteen years. Is it real?"

"It is. Archie?"

Serving liquid refreshment to a group of invited guests can be a pleasant chore, but it wasn't that time. When I asked Mrs. Jerome to name it she only glowered at me, but by the time I had filled Cherry's order for scotch and soda, and supplied Hatch with a liberal dose of Korbeloff, no dilution, and Leo had said he would take bourbon and water, his mother muttered that she would have that too. As I was pouring the bourbon I wondered where we would go from there. It looked as if the time had come for Wolfe to pass on the information which I felt I must give the police without delay, which made it difficult because I didn't have any. That had been fine for a bait to get them there, but what now? I suppose Wolfe would have held them somehow, but he didn't have to. He had rung for beer, and Fritz had brought it and was putting the tray on his desk when the doorbell rang. I handed Leo his bourbon and water and went to the hall. Out on the stoop, with his big round face nearly touching the glass, was Inspector Cramer of Homicide.

Wolfe had told me enough, before the company came, to give me a general idea of the program, so the sight of Cramer, just Cramer, was a letdown. But as I went down the hall other figures appeared, none of them strangers, and that looked better. In fact it looked fine. I swung the door wide and in they came —Cramer, then Saul Panzer, then Margot Dickey,

51

then Alfred Kiernan, and, bringing up the rear, Sergeant Purley Stebbins. By the time I had the door closed and bolted they had their coats off, including Cramer, and it was also fine to see that he expected to stay a while. Ordinarily, once in, he marches down the hall and into the office without ceremony, but that time he waved the others ahead, including me, and he and Stebbins came last, herding us in. Crossing the sill, I stepped aside for the pleasure of seeing his face when his eyes lit on those already there and the empty chairs waiting. Undoubtedly he had expected to find Wolfe alone, reading a book. He came in two paces, glared around, fastened the glare on Wolfe, and barked, "What's all this?"

"I was expecting you," Wolfe said politely. "Miss Quon, if you don't mind moving, Mr. Cramer likes that chair. Good evening, Miss Dickey. Mr. Kiernan, Mr. Stebbins. If you will all be seated—"

"Panzer!" Cramer barked. Saul, who had started for a chair in the rear, stopped and turned.

"I'm running this," Cramer declared. "Panzer, you're under arrest and you'll stay with Stebbins and keep your mouth shut. I don't want—"

"No," Wolfe said sharply. "If he's under arrest take him out of here. You are not running this, not in my house. If you have warrants for anyone present, or have taken them by lawful police power, take them and leave these premises. Would you bulldoze me, Mr. Cramer? You should know better."

That was the point, Cramer did know him. There was the stage, all set. There were Mrs. Jerome and Leo and Cherry and Emil Hatch, and the empty chairs, and above all, there was the fact that he had been expected. He wouldn't have taken Wolfe's word for that; he wouldn't have taken Wolfe's word for anything; but whenever he appeared on our stoop *not* expected I always left the chain-bolt on until he had stated his business and I had reported to Wolfe. And if he had been expected there was no telling what Wolfe had ready to spring. So Cramer gave up the bark and merely growled, "I want to talk with you."

"Certainly." Wolfe indicated the red leather chair, which Cherry had vacated. "Be seated."

"Not here. Alone."

Wolfe shook his head. "It would be a waste of time. This way is better and quicker. You know quite well, sir, it was a mistake to barge in here and roar at me that you are running my house. Either go, with whomever you can lawfully take, or sit down while I tell you who killed Kurt Bottweill." Wolfe wiggled a finger. "Your chair."

Cramer's round red face had been redder than normal from the outside cold, and now was redder still. He glanced around, compressed his lips until he didn't have any, and went to the red leather chair and sat.

VIII

Wolfe sent his eyes around as I circled to my desk. Saul had got to a chair in the rear after all, but Stebbins had too and was at his elbow. Margot had passed in front of the Jeromes and Emil Hatch to get to the chair at the end nearest me, and Cherry and Al Kiernan were at the other end, a little back of the others. Hatch had finished his Korbeloff and put the glass on the floor, but Cherry and the Jeromes were hanging on to their tall ones.

Wolfe's eyes came to rest on Cramer and he spoke. "I must confess that I stretched it a little. I can't tell you, at the moment, who killed Bottweill; I have only a supposition; but soon I can, and will. First some facts for you. I assume you know that for the past two months Mr. Goodwin has been seeing something of Miss Dickey. He says she dances well."

"Yeah." Cramer's voice came over sandpaper of the roughest grit. "You can save that for later. I want to know if you sent Panzer to meet—"

Wolfe cut him off. "You will. I'm headed for that. But you may prefer this firsthand. Archie, if you please. What Miss Dickey asked you to do last Monday evening, and what happened."

I cleared my throat. "We were dancing at the Flamingo Club. She said Bottweill had been telling her for a year that he would marry her next week, but next week never came, and she was going to have a showdown with him. She asked me to get a blank marriage license and fill it out for her and me and give it to her, and she would show it to Bottweill and tell him now or

54

never. I got the blank on Tuesday, and filled it in, and Wednesday I gave it to her."

I stopped. Wolfe prompted me. "And yesterday afternoon?"

"She told me that the license trick had worked perfectly. That was about a minute before Bottweill entered the studio. I said in my statement to the District Attorney that she told me Bottweill was going to marry her, but I didn't mention the license. It was immaterial."

"Did she tell you what had happened to the license?"

So we were emptying the bag. I nodded. "She said Bottweill had torn it up and put the pieces in the wastebasket by the desk in his office. The night before. Thursday evening."

"And what did you do when you went to the office after Bottweill had died?"

"I dumped the wastebasket and put the stuff back in it, piece by piece. No part of the license was there."

"You made sure of that?"

"Yes."

Wolfe left me and asked Cramer, "Any questions?"

"No. He lied in his statement. I'll attend to that later. What I want—"

Margot Dickey blurted, "Then Cherry took it!" She craned her neck to see across the others. "You took it, you slut!"

"I did not." The steel was in Cherry's chirp again. Her eyes didn't leave Wolfe, and she told him, "I'm not going to wait any longer—"

"Miss Quon!" he snapped. "I'm doing this." He returned to Cramer. "Now another fact. Yesterday I had a luncheon appointment with Mr. Bottweill at Rusterman's restaurant. He had once dined at my table and wished to reciprocate. Shortly before I left to keep the appointment he phoned to ask me to do him a favor. He said he was extremely busy and might be a few minutes late, and he needed a pair of white cotton gloves, medium size, for a man, and would I stop at some shop on the way and get them. It struck me as a

55

peculiar request, but he was a peculiar man. Since Mr. Goodwin had chores to do, and I will not ride in taxi-cabs if there is any alternative, I had engaged a car at Baxter's, and the chauffeur recommended a shop on Eighth Avenue between Thirty-ninth and Fortieth Streets. We stopped there and I bought the gloves."

Cramer's eyes were such narrow slits that none of the blue-gray showed. He wasn't buying any part of it, which was unjustified, since some of it was true.

Wolfe went on. "At the lunch table I gave the gloves to Mr. Bottweill, and he explained, somewhat vaguely, what he wanted them for. I gathered that he had taken pity on some vagabond he had seen on a park bench, and had hired him to serve refreshments at his office party, costumed as Santa Claus, and had decided that the only way to make his hands presentable was to have him wear gloves. You shake your head, Mr. Cramer?"

"You're damn right I do. You would have reported that. No reason on earth not to. Go ahead and finish."

"I'll finish this first. I didn't report it because I thought you would find the murderer without it. It was practically certain that the vagabond had merely ske-daddled out of fright, since he couldn't possibly have known of the jar of poison in the workshop, not to mention other considerations. And as you know, I have a strong aversion to involvement in matters where I have no concern or interest. You can of course check this—with the staff at Rusterman's, my presence there with Mr. Bottweill, and with the chauffeur, my conferring with him about the gloves and our stopping at the shop to buy them."

"You're reporting it now."

"I am indeed." Wolfe was unruffled. "Because I understood from Mr. Goodwin that you were extending and intensifying your search for the man who was there as Santa Claus, and with your army and your resources it probably wouldn't take you long when the holiday had ended to learn where the gloves were bought and get a description of the man who bought them. My physique is not unique, but it is—uncommon, and the only question was how long it would

56

take you to get to me, and then I would be under inquisition. Obviously I had to report the episode to you and suffer your rebuke for not reporting it earlier, but I wanted to make it as tolerable as possible. I had one big advantage: I knew that the man who acted Santa Claus was almost certainly not the murderer, and I decided to use it. I needed first to have a talk with one of those people, and I did so, with Miss Quon, who came here last evening."

"Why Miss Quon?"

Wolfe turned a hand over. "When I have finished you can decide whether such details are important. With her I discussed her associates at that place and their relationships, and I became satisfied that Bottweill had in fact decided to marry her. That was all. You can also decide later whether it is worth while to ask her to corroborate that, and I have no doubt she will."

He was looking at Cherry, of course, for any sign of danger. She had started to blurt it out once, and might again. But, meeting his gaze, she didn't move a muscle.

Wolfe returned to Cramer. "This morning I acted. Mr. Goodwin was absent, at the District Attorney's office, so I called in Mr. Panzer. After spending an hour with me here he went to do some errands. The first one was to learn whether Bottweill's wastebasket had been emptied since his conversation with Miss Dickey in his office Thursday evening. As you know, Mr. Panzer is highly competent. Through Miss Quon he got the name and address of the cleaning woman, found her and talked with her, and was told that the wastebasket had been emptied at about six o'clock Thursday afternoon and not since then. Meanwhile I—"

"Cherry took it—the pieces," Margot said.

Wolfe ignored her. "Meanwhile I was phoning everyone concerned—Mrs. Jerome and her son, Miss Dickey, Miss Quon, Mr. Hatch, and Mr. Kiernan—and inviting them to come here for a conference at six-fifteen. I told them that Mr. Goodwin had information which he intended to give the police, which

57

was not true, and that I thought it best to discuss it first with them."

"I told you so," Hatch muttered.

Wolfe ignored him too. "Mr. Panzer's second errand, or series of errands, was the delivery of some messages. He had written them in longhand, at my dictation here this morning, on plain sheets of paper, and had addressed plain envelopes. They were identical and ran as follows:

"When I was there yesterday putting on my costume I saw you through a crack in the door and I saw what you did. Do you want me to tell the cops? Be at Grand Central information booth upper level at 6:30 today. I'll come up to you and say 'Saint Nick.'"

"By God," Cramer said, "you admit it."

Wolfe nodded. "I proclaim it. The messages were signed 'Santa Claus.' Mr. Panzer accompanied the messenger who took them to the persons I have named, and made sure they were delivered. They were not so much shots at random as they may appear. If one of those people had killed Bottweill it was extremely likely that the poison had been put in the bottle while the vagabond was donning the Santa Claus costume; Miss Quon had told me, as no doubt she has told you, that Bottweill invariably took a drink of Pernod when he returned from lunch; and, since the appearance of Santa Claus at the party had been a surprise to all of them, and none of them knew who he was, it was highly probable that the murderer would believe he had been observed and would be irresistibly impelled to meet the writer of the message. So it was a reasonable assumption that one of the shots would reach its target. The question was, which one?"

Wolfe stopped to pour beer. He did pour it, but I suspected that what he really stopped for was to offer an opening for comment or protest. No one had any, not even Cramer. They all just sat and gazed at him. I was thinking that he had neatly skipped one detail:

that the message from Santa Claus had not gone to Cherry Quon. She knew too much about him.

Wolfe put the bottle down and turned to go on to Cramer. "There was the possibility, of course, that more than one of them would go to you with the message, but even if you decided, because it had been sent to more than one, that it was some hoax, you would want to know who perpetrated it, and you would send one of them to the rendezvous under surveillance. Any one or more, excepting the murderer, might go to you, or none might; and surely only the murderer would go to the rendezvous without first consulting you. So if one of those six people was guilty, and if it had been possible for Santa Claus to observe him, disclosure seemed next to certain. Saul, you may now report. What happened? You were in the vicinity of the information booth shortly before six-thirty?"

Necks were twisted for a view of Saul Panzer. He nodded. "Yes, sir. At six-twenty. Within three minutes I had recognized three Homicide men scattered around in different spots. I don't know if they recognized me or not. At six twenty-eight I saw Alfred Kiernan walk up near the booth and stand there, about ten feet away from it. I was just about to go and speak to him when I saw Margot Dickey coming up from the Forty-second Street side. She approached to within thirty feet of the booth and stood looking around. Following your instructions in case more than one of them appeared and Miss Dickey was one of them, I went to her and said, 'Saint Nick.' She said, 'Who are you and what do you want?' I said, 'Excuse me, I'll be right back,' and went over to Alfred Kiernan and said to him, 'Saint Nick.' As soon as I said that he raised a hand to his ear, and then here they came, the three I had recognized and two more, and then Inspector Cramer and Sergeant Stebbins. I was afraid Miss Dickey would run, and she did start to, but they had seen me speak to her, and two of them stopped her and had her."

Saul halted because of an interruption. Purley Stebbins, seated next to him, got up and stepped over to

59

Margot Dickey and stood there behind her chair. To me it seemed unnecessary, since I was sitting not much more than arm's length from her and might have been trusted to grab her if she tried to start anything, but Purley is never very considerate of other people's feelings, especially mine.

Saul resumed, "Naturally it was Miss Dickey I was interested in, since they had moved in on a signal from Kiernan. But they had her, so that was okay. They took us to a room back of the parcel room and started in on me, and I followed your instructions. I told them I would answer no questions, would say nothing whatever, except in the presence of Nero Wolfe, because I was acting under your orders. When they saw I meant it they took us out to two police cars and brought us here. Anything else?"

"No," Wolfe told him. "Satisfactory." He turned to Cramer. "I assume Mr. Panzer is correct in concluding that Mr. Kiernan gave your men a signal. So Mr. Kiernan had gone to you with the message?"

"Yes." Cramer had taken a cigar from his pocket and was squeezing it in his hand. He does that sometimes when he would like to squeeze Wolfe's throat instead. "So had three of the others—Mrs. Jerome, her son, and Hatch."

"But Miss Dickey hadn't?"

"No. Neither had Miss Quon."

"Miss Quon was probably reluctant, understandably. She told me last evening that the police's ideas of Orientals are very primitive. As for Miss Dickey, I may say that I am not surprised. For a reason that does not concern you, I am even a little gratified. I have told you that she told Mr. Goodwin that Bottweill had torn up the marriage license and put the pieces in his wastebasket, and they weren't there when Mr. Goodwin looked for them, and the wastebasket hadn't been emptied since early Thursday evening. It was difficult to conceive a reason for anyone to fish around in the wastebasket to remove those pieces, so presumably Miss Dickey lied; and if she lied about the license, the rest of what she told Mr. Goodwin was under suspicion."

Wolfe upturned a palm. "Why would she tell him that Bottweill was going to marry her if it wasn't true? Surely a stupid thing to do, since he would inevitably learn the truth. But it wasn't so stupid if she knew that Bottweill would soon die; indeed it was far from stupid if she had already put the poison in the bottle; it would purge her of motive, or at least help. It was a fair surmise that at their meeting in his office Thursday evening Bottweill had told her, not that he would marry her, but that he had decided to marry Miss Quon, and she decided to kill him and proceeded to do so. And it must be admitted that she would probably never have been exposed but for the complications injected by Santa Claus and my resulting intervention. Have you any comment, Miss Dickey?"

Cramer left his chair, commanding her, "Don't answer! I'm running this now," but she spoke.

"Cherry took those pieces from the wastebasket! She did it! She killed him!" She started up, but Purley had her arm and Cramer told her, moving for her, "She didn't go there to meet a blackmailer, and you did. Look in her bag, Purley. I'll watch her."

61

IX

Cherry Quon was back in the red leather chair. The others had gone, and she and Wolfe and I were alone. They hadn't put cuffs on Margot Dickey, but Purley had kept hold of her arm as they crossed the threshold, with Cramer right behind. Saul Panzer, no longer in custody, had gone along by request. Mrs. Jerome and Leo had been the first to leave. Kiernan had asked Cherry if he could take her home, but Wolfe had said no, he wanted to speak with her privately, and Kiernan and Hatch had left together, which showed a fine Christmas spirit, since Hatch had made no exceptions when he said he despised all of them.

Cherry was on the edge of the chair, spine straight, hands together in her lap. "You didn't do it the way I said," she chirped, without steel.

"No," Wolfe agreed, "but I did it." He was curt. "You ignored one complication, the possibility that you had killed Bottweill yourself. I didn't, I assure you. I couldn't very well send you one of the notes from Santa Claus, under the circumstances; but if those notes had flushed no prey, if none of them had gone to the rendezvous without first notifying the police, I would have assumed that you were guilty and would have proceeded to expose you. How, I don't know; I let that wait on the event; and now that Miss Dickey has taken the bait and betrayed herself it doesn't matter."

Her eyes had widened. "You really thought I might have killed Kurt?"

"Certainly. A woman capable of trying to blackmail me to manufacture evidence of murder would be capable of anything. And, speaking of evidence, while there can be no certainty about a jury's decision when a personable young woman is on trial for murder, now that Miss Dickey is manifestly guilty you may be sure that Mr. Cramer will dig up all he can get, and there should be enough. That brings me to the point I wanted to speak about. In the quest for evidence you will all be questioned, exhaustively and repeatedly. It will—"

"We wouldn't," Cherry put in, "if you had done it the way I said. That would have been proof."

"I preferred my way." Wolfe, having a point to make, was controlling himself. "It will be an ordeal for you. They will question you at length about your talk with Bottweill yesterday morning at breakfast, wanting to know all that he said about his meeting with Miss Dickey in his office Thursday evening, and under the pressure of inquisition you might inadvertently let something slip regarding what he told you about Santa Claus. If you do they will certainly follow it up. I strongly advise you to avoid making such a slip. Even if they believe you, the identity of Santa Claus is no longer important, since they have the murderer, and if they come to me with such a tale I'll have no great difficulty dealing with it."

He turned a hand over. "And in the end they probably won't believe you. They'll think you invented it for some cunning and obscure purpose—as you say, you are an Oriental—and all you would get for it would be more questions. They might even suspect that you were somehow involved in the murder itself. They are quite capable of unreasonable suspicions. So I suggest these considerations as much on your behalf as on mine. I think you will be wise to forget about Santa Claus."

She was eying him, straight and steady. "I like to be wise," she said.

"I'm sure you do, Miss Quon."

"I still think you should have done it my way, but it's done now. Is that all?"

He nodded. "That's all."

She looked at me, and it took a second for me to realize that she was smiling at me. I thought it wouldn't

63

hurt to smile back, and did. She left the chair and came to me, extending a hand, and I arose and took it. She looked up at me.

"I would like to shake hands with Mr. Wolfe, but I know he doesn't like to shake hands. You know, Mr. Goodwin, it must be a very great pleasure to work for a man as clever as Mr. Wolfe. So extremely clever. It has been very exciting to be here. Now I say good-by."

She turned and went.

Easter
Parade

I

I swiveled my chair to face Nero Wolfe directly across the expanse of his desk top, and to look him in the eye. Then I made a speech.

"Nothing doing. If you wanted me to hook something really worth while, like a Mogok ruby, I might consider it, but I am not an orchid snatcher. For what you pay me I do your mail, I make myself obnoxious to people, I tail them when necessary, I shoot when I have to and get shot at, I stick around and take every mood you've got, I give you and Theodore a hand in the plant rooms when required, I lie to Inspector Cramer and Sergeant Stebbins whether required or not, I even help Fritz in the kitchen in emergencies, I answer the phone. I could go on and on. But I will not grab an orchid from a female bosom in the Easter parade. There is—"

"I haven't asked you to," Wolfe snapped. He wiggled a finger at me. "You assumed I was headed for that, but you were wrong. I only said I wanted to hire someone for such an errand—someone adroit, discreet, resolute, and reliable."

"Me, then," I insisted.

"Pfui. Granting that you qualify, you are not unique. I would pay him a hundred dollars, another hundred if successful, and all expenses if a predicament results."

My brows went up. "Wow. Maybe I'm not unique, but the orchid must be."

"It is." The seventh of a ton of him came forward in his custom-built chair. "Mr. Millard Bynoe has produced a flamingo-pink Vanda—both petals and sepals true pink, with no tints, spots, or edgings."

67

"Hooray!"

"But I don't believe it. I have it from Mr. Lewis Hewitt, who had it from his gardener, who had it from Mr. Bynoe's gardener, but I don't believe it. As you know, I have been hybridizing for a pink Vanda for years, and have come no closer to it than the rose-lilac of peetersiana or the magenta of sandarae. I don't believe it, and I have to see it."

"Then phone Bynoe and arrange it. You won't leave the house on business, but this isn't business, it's an acute attack of incurable envy. I'll go along to watch your face—"

"I *have* phoned him. He cordially invited me to visit his collection at my convenience, at his place on Long Island, but he wouldn't admit that he has a pink Vanda, so I wouldn't see it. According to Mr. Hewitt, he intends to display it in its full glory at the International Flower Show next year, but that is too long to wait. No one has seen it but Mr. Bynoe himself, his wife, and his gardener. But—also from Mr. Hewitt—his wife has persuaded him to let her wear a spray of it on Easter Day. They will attend Easter service at Saint Thomas's Church. That will provide an opportunity, if not to inspect the plant, at least to see the bloom."

"It sure will," I agreed enthusiastically. "You've never been in an Easter parade and it will be a treat for you. Only you ought to have a new suit and hat, and it's only five days—"

I stopped because he wasn't reacting properly. Instead of scowling or growling, or both, he was merely nodding thoughtfully, as if the idea of rubbing elbows, not to mention other parts of his anatomy, with his fellow beings in the Fifth Avenue Easter mob wasn't repellent at all. Envy broadens a man.

"It wouldn't do," he declared. "If I could plant myself in front of her for a prolonged scrutiny . . ." His shoulders went up and down. "No. I must examine them at leisure, at least one of them, and with a glass. I wouldn't expect you to do it. Nor Saul. Orrie?"

I shook my head. "I doubt it. Not just for the two Cs, but he might as a personal favor for you."

He made a face. "I won't solicit a favor."

68

"Okay. There isn't time to put an ad in the paper for an experienced orchid snatcher. Do you want me to scare one up?"

"I do."

"Then I'll scout around. I have a prospect in mind —in fact, two. But forget about the predicament expenses. The predicament, if any, will be up to him. A C for the try, and another C if he gets the spray or a usable part of it. Right?"

"Yes." Wolfe was frowning. But if he fails—" He aimed the frown at me. "You have a color camera."

"*You* have," I corrected him. "You paid for it. I use it on occasion."

"I suggest that you may regard this as an occasion. Your Sundays are your own when we are not engaged on an important case, but you may take some other day instead. Aren't there dozens of people with cameras up and down Fifth Avenue in that pandemonium?"

"Not dozens. Thousands."

He turned a hand over. "Well?"

"Uh-huh." I considered it. "I admit he might flub it, and I admit I could get a picture, though I can't say how true the color would be. Pinks are tricky. But I guess it's no go, because as you say, my Sundays are mine, and I would do it only as a personal favor for you, and you won't solicit a favor. Too bad."

"I should have qualified that. There are only four people of whom I would ask a favor, and Orrie is not one of them. You are."

"Then go ahead and ask. Call me Mr. Goodwin."

His lips tightened. "Mr. Goodwin," he said coldly, "I solicit a favor."

It's amazing what lengths a man will go to for envy.

II

Easter Sunday the weather wasn't perfect, but I had seen much worse. As, shortly before noon, I left the old brownstone, the sun was slanting down into West Thirty-fifth Street, and I crossed over to have it on me. The breeze from the river wasn't as chilly as I had expected, and I unbuttoned my topcoat. I was not arrayed, merely had my clothes on, with the Centrex, loaded and ready, dangling from a strap over my shoulder.

Crosstown to Fifth Avenue, and uptown for five blocks, it was just a pleasant walk with plenty of room, but in front of the library some early birds were already around, moving or standing in the sunshine, and I had to start dodging. From there on it got thicker all the way, and it was a good thing I had allowed extra time, since I had told Tabby I would be in front of Saint Thomas's at twelve-thirty.

Tabby will do for him, though I know his name and address. Tabby will do. It had been a mistake to bait him with two Cs, one down and one if and when, since a pair of twenties would have been more his speed, and it might make him nervous, but I had followed orders. I had briefed him thoroughly, shown him pictures of Millard Bynoe and his wife, and even introduced Vanda to him by giving him a spray, though not flamingo-pink, from one of Wolfe's plants. There would be a lot of bosoms sporting orchids in that stampede, from Cattleyas to Calanthes. Also, to cinch it, I was going to give him a sign.

By the time I reached Saint Patrick's at Fiftieth Street, with three blocks to go, the street was no better than the sidewalks—absolutely solid with dressed-up bipeds, some of them looking pleased and even happy. The display of lipstick colors and patterns, goofy hats, and flossy neckties deserved more appreciation than I had time for as I wormed my way north, rubbing not only elbows but shoulders and hips. As I pushed through to the curb in front of Saint Thomas's, I was thinking it might be worth while to come back next year on my own time for a thorough survey of the panorama, provided I could rent a suit of armor at a bargain. At Fifty-second Street a six-foot amazon in a purple ensemble had got me in the ribs.

I stretched my own six feet by rising on my toes and spotted Tabby, anchored out of the current in a niche flanking the church entrance. He was a little squirt, several inches under six feet, but I got enough of him to see that the C I had given him had gone down the drain for a new topcoat, a gray plaid, and a new hat, a classy gray snap-brim. The true Easter-parade spirit, I thought, and grinned at him when I caught his eye. It wasn't necessary to shove through to him, since he had been well briefed.

I needed a vantage point for aiming as they came out of the church, and there it was beside me—a wooden box there on the sidewalk at the edge of the curb, some sixteen inches high, just the elevation I needed. But it was occupied. Standing on it was a young woman in a tan woolen belted coat, with a camera in her hand held at breast level as she faced downtown, scanning the rabble as it shuffled along. I touched her elbow and she looked down at me. I gave her my best smile, which was no strain after one glimpse of her face.

"Have you ever," I asked her, "stood on a box with a peer of the realm?"

"Certainly," she declared. "Don't bother me, I'm busy." She went back to scanning.

I directed my voice up to her ear. "But you have never stood on a box with a prince of the blood, and this is your chance. My grandmother, the queen dowager, is coming out of that church and I want to get a shot of her. I'll stand on the edge and I won't jostle."

71

She was facing down again. "I hate to refuse, Your Highness, but it's not my box. It was lent me by a grandee, and he would—"

"Hey, Archie Goodwin!"

The voice came from behind, and I turned. There was another box at the curb, two paces along, and beyond it still another. On them were men with cameras, and straddling the gap, with his left foot on one box and his right on the other, was a third man with a camera, grinning at me.

He spoke. "You don't remember me."

"Sure I do. The *Gazette*. Joe. Joe Merrick—no, wait a minute—Herrick. Joe Herrick. Did you lend this lady the box she's on?"

"Yeah, who wouldn't? Look at her!"

"I have. Any objection if she shares it with me?"

"That's up to her. I'd rather she shared it with me, but you had the idea first. What are you after? Where's the corpse?"

"No corpse. I'm just practicing." I turned to tell her I had cleared it with the grandee, but at that moment all four of them brought their cameras up to their chins, facing the church entrance. The exodus had started. I planted my left foot on the edge of her box, heaved myself up, and caught the edge of the next-door box with my right foot with a fancy spread-eagle. It was too near a split to be comfortable, but at least I was up high enough to focus over the heads of the crowd. A glance showed me that Tabby had left his niche and edged through to the line of exit.

Out they came, all flavors. The men ran from cutaways to sacks and from toppers to floppies, not more than half of them with topcoats, and the women displayed an assortment of furs, coats, jackets, stoles, suits, and hats for the birds. I shot a couple to warm up the camera, and once I thought I spotted my target, but the man with her was not Millard Bynoe, and as she approached I saw that her orchid spray wasn't Vanda, but Phalaenopsis. Then suddenly there she was, headed straight toward me, with a man on either side of her, and the one on her right was Bynoe. Her fur jacket, sable or long-haired hamster or something, was open, and drooping below her left shoulder was a ten-inch spray of glowing pink. She was one of the most attractive objects I had seen that day, and as she got closer and I aimed the camera for another shot the back of my mind was reflecting that you couldn't find a better argument to persuade a man to marry a woman twenty years his junior, which was what Millard Bynoe had done.

Having given Tabby a sign, I had the camera to my eye again, so I didn't actually see all of what happened in the next two seconds, but I can show one instant of it, the instant I pressed the button, with four pictures I took of her. I had warned Tabby not to try for the spray while cameras were on her, as I knew they would be as she left the church, and of course her having an escort at each elbow made it impossible to sneak up from the side, but evidently the vision of another C was too much for him, and he had worked his way around to get at her from the front. Seeing his head and arm in the finder, and the arm and hand of the man on Mrs. Bynoe's left warding him off, I lowered the camera, slid off the boxes, and started forward with the notion of grabbing his coattail and jerking him away, but he had wriggled off before I got there. Mrs. Bynoe was looking upset, with her teeth clamped on her lip, and her escorts were asking her questions, but she shook her head, said something to her husband, and turned uptown, the men close beside her. The pink spray was intact.

I looked around, over shoulders and between hats, saw Tabby making himself small against the railing, and saw him move, uptown. The nervy little cuss was stalking his prey. It wouldn't have been discreet to chat with him there in the public eye, even if I had anything helpful to say, and anyway it was understood that he was strictly on his own, but there was nothing against my being an impartial observer. So I tagged along, some eight rows of hats behind Tabby and fifteen or so behind the trio.

They took their time. Of course Fifth Avenue was closed to traffic, but one of the Bynoe limousines was probably parked nearby on Madison, so Tabby didn't have all day. At Fifty-fourth Street they headed across the avenue, and that was slow going since they kept three abreast. By the time they reached the other curb Tabby had closed in to eight or ten feet, and I was keeping my distance from Tabby.

It happened when they had gone some fifty yards along Fifty-fourth Street, about halfway to Madison. The throng wasn't as thick there as on the avenue, but it was still a throng. Tabby was almost directly behind them, and I wasn't far off, when suddenly Mrs. Bynoe stopped short, grabbed her husband's arms, and said to him in a sort of half-strangled scream, "I can't stand it! I didn't want to—here on the street—I can't breathe! Mil, you—" She let go of his arms, straightened up, rigid, shuddered all over, and toppled. The two men had her before she went down, but then she went into convulsion, her neck and spine arching backward and she got away from them and was on the sidewalk.

Tabby darted in from the circle of bystanders, snatched the pink spray from her shoulder, darted out again, through the circle, and sprinted for Madison Avenue.

There was only one thing for me to do, and I did it. I went after him. For one thing, if anyone else felt like chasing him, my being ahead would show him he wasn't needed. For another, I couldn't have asked for a better excuse to make myself scarce. So I stretched my legs, and while I can no longer do the hundred in 10:7, I can move. So could Tabby. When he got to Madison I was still ten steps behind. He took the corner, turning downtown, without slackening, and ran into luck. Twenty yards down a taxi was discharging a couple of passengers. Tabby was there before they shut the door, and I was too. He tumbled in, and while I didn't tumble, I didn't dwadle. The hackie, swiveling his neck for a look, inquired mildly, "Ghosts?"

I controlled my panting enough to speak. "Right. My friend here had never been in a church before, and the choir's costumes got him. Nine-eighteen West Thirty-fifth Street."

He surveyed the street to the rear, saw no cop or

other pursuer coming for fugitives, turned and pulled the gear lever, and we rolled. When we had gone a block Tabby opened his mouth to speak, but I glared at him and he shut it again. Hackies usually have good ears, sometimes too good, and it wouldn't help to give that one any items to remember us by. It was already bad enough. So he had heard nothing, because there was nothing for him to hear, when he deposited us at the curb in front of the old brownstone. I led the way up the seven steps of the stoop, let us in with my key, got my hat and coat on the hall rack and shelf, and was going to do likewise with Tabby's, but he hung on to his coat, carefully inserted his hand in the left side pocket, and carefully withdrew it with thumb and fore-finger closed on the stem of the spray.

"Here it is," he said. "Come across. I'm on my way."

"Hold your horses. I have to tap the till." I put his coat on a hanger and his hat on the shelf, steered him across the hall and into the front room, told him to wait, opened the soundproofed door to the office, passed through, and shut it behind me.

Wolfe, at his desk with sections of the Sunday paper scattered around, looked up, saw I was empty-handed except for the camera, and demanded, "Well?"

I crossed to my desk and put the camera down, and stood. "Yes, sir. I got pictures, and he got the spray. But first I want—"

"Where is it?"

"Just a minute. He's in the front room with it, hanging on to it until he sees his money, and as soon as I pay him he'll want to skip, and there's a complication. Mrs. Bynoe collapsed on the sidewalk, in convulsion, and while she was lying there with her head curved back nearly to her heels he dashed in and grabbed the spray and ran. It wasn't a pretty performance and I would have liked to collar him and call a cop, but that wouldn't have helped her any, and also there was you to consider, sitting here with your mouth watering. So I ran after him. If I had caught him in time I would have walked him here, but before I reached him he had hopped a taxi. There was no use—"

"I want to see the spray."

"Just a minute. We may—"

"There will be many minutes. Get him in here."

I let him have his way because he wasn't listening anyhow. I went to the front room and brought Tabby. When he got to Wolfe's desk and Wolfe extended a hand, I thought Tabby was going to refuse to part with it until he touched the money, and so did he, but Wolfe growled like a lion at sight of a hunk of juicy meat, and Tabby handed him the spray, which had been crushed some, but not badly. Half of the dozen or so blossoms were intact. Wolfe looked them over, one by one, and then got a magnifiying glass from a drawer and went over them again, with his lips closed so tight he didn't have any. Finally he pushed his chair back, arose, and, holding the spray by the butt of the stem, made for the hall and the kitchen, where there were two refrigerators, one cool and one cold. Soon he returned, without the spray, crossed to his desk and sat, and announced, "I would give three thousand dollars for that plant."

I shook my head. "Don't look at me. No, thanks. And if you want to deal with Tabby, deal direct. Before I pay him I would like to report in detail, if and when you've got yourself enough under control to listen."

"Pfui. Have you ever seen me out of control?"

"We can save that. Remind me some time. Sit down, Tabby." I took the chair at my desk and proceeded to report, covering everything, which didn't take long since no long conversations were involved. Apparently Wolfe was taking it in.

I ended up, "It depends on Mrs. Bynoe. As far as I know it could have been epilepsy. But if it was something else, something that gets the cops on it and makes them work, they'll learn that the guy who tried to get at her in front of the church was the one who grabbed the orchids later, and they'll probably find him. When they do, will he talk? Yes. Sooner or later, and I suspect sooner. So I think we might invite Tabby to stick around until we know the score." I looked at my wristwatch. "It's been over an hour. I can try Lon Cohen at the *Gazette*."

Wolfe was frowning at me. "Do so."

I swiveled and dialed. Usually I can get right through to Lon, but that time it took five minutes. When I finally got him he said he was in a boil and I made it snappy.

"A question, maybe two. Have you anything in about Mrs. Millard Bynoe?"

"Yes. She's dead. That's the boil. And last Wednesday you were here collecting pictures of her and her husband. I was just going to ring you. Where do you come in? And Nero Wolfe? Speak."

"At present I'm just curious, and this call is absolutely off the record. If and when we do come in I'll think of you. Where and when did she die, and what killed her?"

"On the sidewalk on Fifty-fourth Street between Madison and Fifth, about an hour ago. What, I don't know, but they have taken the body to the morgue and the Commissioner is standing by, not to mention others. Are you going to open up or not?"

"I'm just curious. It itches. You might ring me every hour on the hour."

He said sure, he had nothing else to do, and hung up. I turned and relayed it to Wolfe, and as I finished Tabby was out of his chair, his sharp little eyes darting from Wolfe to me and back again.

"I want my money," he said, tending to squeak. "That's what I want, see?" He started to tremble. "What the hell!"

I went and put a hand on his shoulder, friendly. "Take it easy, Tabby," I told him. I turned to Wolfe. "I met this gentleman a couple of years ago in connection with one of our cases, and did him a little favor, but he doesn't know my true character, or yours either. He suspects we may be tying a can on him, and he's scared stiff, and you can't blame him. Maybe he scares easy, but he has been around, and he knows they wouldn't call the Commissioner in on Easter Sunday unless they had something, even for Mrs. Millard Bynoe, and I know it too. Ten to one it's murder, and if so they'll find Tabby, and if they find him they'll find me, and if they find me they'll find you."

Wolfe was glaring at us. "Confound it," he muttered.

"Yeah," I agreed. "So you and Tabby have problems, not to mention me. You hired him, through me, to commit petty larceny, and that will make fine reading. He committed the larceny, but what's worse, he has now got it in his head that we have framed him for something in a murder, and try to get it out. He's too scared to listen to reason. You may think of something besides reason for him to listen to."

"Is there any chance that he seized an opportunity? When he got in front of her as she crossed the sidewalk?"

"No. Cross it off. I saw it. And why? Skip it. Also, I know him and that's not in him."

"Who is he? What's his name?"

"Just call him Tabby. He prefers it."

"I want my money," Tabby squeaked. "That's all I want."

Wolfe, eying him, took in air, clear down, and let it out again. "You understand, sir," he said, "that this may be only a bugaboo. Mrs. Bynoe may have died of natural causes."

"I want my money," Tabby squeaked.

"No doubt. But she may not, and in that case the investigation will be thorough. We'll soon know, and if it was murder I'm in a pickle. Putting it at a minimum, I would prefer not to have it published that I hired a man to steal a flower, especially if he tore it from her breast as she lay dying. You want your money. If I give it to you, and you leave, what will happen? Either you will spend it in an effort to keep yourself out of the hands of the police, not an attractive prospect for you; or you will go to the police at once and unburden yourself, not an attractive prospect for me."

Wolfe sighed again. "So I'm not going to pay you, not— Let me finish, please. I shall not pay you now. There is a comfortable room on the third floor of this house, and my cook is unsurpassed if not unequaled. If you will occupy that room, communicate with no

78

one, and not leave the house until I give the word, I will then pay you the hundred dollars and also ten dollars for each day you have been here."

During the next minute Tabby opened his mouth three times to speak and each time closed it again. It was a hard chew for him, and when he finally got to the point of words they were not for Wolfe. He turned to me and demanded, "What about this guy?"

I grinned at him. "He could lie rings around you, Tabby. But he's too damn conceited to double-cross a man, let alone a peanut. Also, if I count, I'll sign it."

He left me to squint at Wolfe, and after another chew he nodded. "Okay, but no lousy ten bucks a day. Twenty."

As I mentioned, the offer of two Cs had been a mistake. Delusions of grandeur. Wolfe, being in a pickle, would probably have stood for it, but I put in. "Nothing doing," I said firmly. "Ten a day and found, and wait till you taste the found." I touched his elbow. "Come on and I'll show you your room."

III

Five hours later, at seven-eighteen that evening, I went to answer the doorbell and found Inspector Cramer on the stoop. Since Lon Cohen had phoned around four o'clock to say that Mrs. Bynoe had been murdered, and to ask for copy, which he didn't get, I had expected company sooner, but of course it had taken a little time for them to get a line on the photographers who had had box seats, or stands, in front of the church.

Tabby had chosen to lunch in his room from a tray instead of joining us in the dining room, but afterward he had relaxed enough to go with me to the basement to shoot some pool, and I spent the rest of the afternoon there with him, with time out for answering three phone calls and for performing a chore I thought advisable, namely, taking the roll of film from the Centrex and locking it in a desk drawer. We were in the basement when the doorbell rang, and I took Tabby up with me and sent him on upstairs before I opened up. Also, seeing Inspector Cramer through the one-way glass panel, I stepped into the office to see that the spray of Vanda wasn't on view and to tell Wolfe who the caller was. He put down the book he was reading and growled.

After letting me take his hat and coat in the hall, which showed that he didn't intend merely to fire a couple of shots and go, Cramer tramped ahead into the office, and when I entered he was seated in the red leather chair near the end of Wolfe's desk and was declining an invitation to have some beer; and as I crossed to my desk he spoke to my back.

80

"You, Goodwin. I want information, and I want it straight and fast. What were you doing in front of Saint Thomas's today?"

I sat and raised my brows. "Why start there? Take the whole day. I woke up at eight o'clock, realized it was not only Sunday but also Easter Sunday, and decided to enjoy—"

"Stop clowning and answer my question!"

"Pfui," Wolfe muttered.

I shook my head at Cramer. "You know better than that. Even when you're worked up, as I can see you are, you still know better. What's the ground?"

His keen blue-gray eyes, looking smaller than they were on account of his big round face, were hard at me. "Damn you," he said, "I'm in a hurry, but I ought to know you by this time. A woman named Mrs. Millard Bynoe left that church today while you were there at the curb taking pictures. Her husband and a man named Frimm were with her. They crossed the avenue and walked east on Fifty-fourth Street, and in the middle of the block she suddenly collapsed and had convulsions, and she died there on the sidewalk. The body was taken to the morgue, and the preliminary report says there are signs of strychnine, and a needle was found in her abdomen. Details of the needle are being withheld, except that it is hollow and it had contained strychnine, and from its size and shape it could have been shot at her by a spring mechanism from a range up to twenty feet, maybe more, depending on the mechanism."

Cramer's eyes darted to Wolfe and back to me. "You want ground. It was approximately twelve minutes—say ten to fifteen—after she left the church that she collapsed on the sidewalk. As she was leaving the church there were at least five cameras aimed at her, five that I know about, and you were aiming one of them. What for?"

I was meeting his eyes. "You've got ground, all right," I conceded. "You asked what I was doing in front of Saint Thomas's today, and you sure have a right to know, so I'll tell you."

I did so, with all details of my words and actions,

except that I didn't mention Tabby or Mrs. Bynoe or orchids, and I didn't include the fact that I had been present when Mrs. Bynoe collapsed. My finale was merely that I had strolled away from the church, to Madison Avenue, and taken a taxi home.

I leaned back. "That's it," I said. "I understand now why you came instead of inviting me down. Naturally you want the camera, and under the circumstances I don't blame you." I swiveled and got the Centrex, in its leather case with the strap, from the desk, and swiveled back. "Here it is. If you want to take it along I'd like a receipt."

He said he certainly wanted to take it along, and I got at the typewriter and wrote a receipt, and he signed it. As I dropped it in a drawer he said that my signed statement should include a declaration that the camera I had given him was the one I had used in front of the church, and I said it would. When I turned back his eyes were leveled at me again.

"How well do you know Joseph Herrick?" he demanded.

"Not very well. I know he's been a *Gazette* photographer for several years. I've met him around a few times, that's all."

"Do you know the other two men there with cameras? Or the girl?"

"No. Never saw any of them before. I don't know their names."

"Did you know Mrs. Bynoe?"

"No. Never saw her either."

"You weren't there for the purpose of aiming a camera at her?"

"At her? No."

"What were you there for?"

I waved a hand. "To take pictures. Like ten thousand of my fellow citizens."

"They weren't all there in front of that church. You understand, Goodwin, the way it looks now, that needle was fired with some kind of a mechanism in one of those cameras that were focused on Mrs. Bynoe. You see things. Did you see anything peculiar about one of those cameras?"

82

"No. I'll give it a thought, but I'm sure I didn't."

"Or anything peculiar about the manner or actions of any of those four people with cameras?"

"No. Again I'll give it a thought, but no. Of course I was taking pictures myself and I wasn't interested in them or their cameras."

Cramer grunted. He regarded me for a long moment and then transferred to Wolfe. "I'll tell you," he said. "I'll just tell you why I came here instead of sending for Goodwin and the camera. Mrs. Bynoe was wearing a bunch of orchids, and her husband says they were very special orchids. There is only one plant in the world, and he has it. While she was lying on the sidewalk, in convulsion, a man darted in from the crowd and snatched the orchids off her and ran. Frimm grabbed his arm but he jerked away. Of course he didn't stick the needle in her then, she was already dying, but that's not the point. The point is that I know how you are on orchids, and that Goodwin was around. The orchids alone, or Goodwin alone, I might pass, but the two together—that's why I'm here. I want to know if you have anything to say, and if so what, and I want to ask some questions."

Wolfe's lips had tightened. "Is it possible," he inquired, "that you are intimating that it was Mr. Goodwin who took the orchids?"

"No. I know he didn't. I have a description of the man who did. But you know damn well how it is when there's a smell of either you or Goodwin within a mile of a murder, and here is Goodwin *and* orchids. Have you anything to say?"

"Yes. I request you to leave my house."

"After you answer some questions." Cramer leaned forward. "Have you any knowledge of the man who took the orchids from Mrs. Bynoe?"

Wolfe put his hands on the edge of his desk, pushed his chair back, and got his bulk upright, on his feet. "Mr. Cramer," he said coldly, "your talent for making yourself offensive is extraordinary. Presumably investigating a murder, you invade my privacy in my home with the preposterous intent of involving me in the theft of a bunch of flowers." He moved, walked halfway to the door, stopped, and turned. "If you wished to question me about your murder I would listen, and would even answer. I know nothing whatever about it. I know nothing about Mrs. Bynoe and I know no one who does, and I have no inkling of any information that could possibly be relevant to her murder. Since you assume that the needle was propelled by a mechansim concealed in one of the cameras, I will add that I also know nothing of any of the persons who were there with cameras, except Mr. Goodwin, and he has told you what he saw and did. If you want to nag him about it, and he cares to submit, there he is."

He walked out. Cramer twisted his neck to watch him go, then twisted it back to give me a look.

"Nag hell," he rasped. "Just a big gob of egomania, and you're not much better. Okay, I'll ask you, have you any knowledge of the man who took the orchids from Mrs. Bynoe?"

I looked apologetic. "I'm sorry, Inspector, but I work for him and—"

"Answer the question!"

"And you know how that is. It's a strain, working for an egomaniac, but it's good pay, and I simply can't risk answering questions he wouldn't answer. What he said about the murder goes for me too, I know absolutely nothing. On other matters, such as my acquaintance with posy snatchers, I have to pass. Look how you offended him."

His eyes were going right through me. "You refuse to answer."

"Certainly. I would also refuse to answer if you asked me if I stole this necktie. That *would* offend Mr. Wolfe. But if—"

"How would you like to come downtown for a session with Lieutenant Rowcliff?"

"I'd love it. I once got him stuttering in eight minutes, the best I ever did, and I'd like—"

I stopped because he was being rude. He arose and, with the camera in his hand and the strap dangling, headed for the door. Thinking he might have an idea of looking for Wolfe, I got up and followed, but in the hall he turned to the front, and, doubting if he would appreciate help with his coat, I merely stood and watched until he had let himself out and banged the door shut. Then I about-faced and went and pushed the swinging door to the kitchen.

It was a pleasant scene, the egomaniac having, as usual, his Sunday-evening snack with the cook. Fritz was on a stool at the long table in the center, steering a dripping endive core to his open mouth. Wolfe, seated at my breakfast table against the wall, was pouring honey on steaming halves of buttermilk biscuits. A glass and a bottle of milk were there, and I went and poured.

I asked where Tabby was and was told that a tray had been taken to his room. Fritz told me there were plenty of biscuits in the warmer, and I thanked him and got a couple.

"You know," I said offhand as I picked up the jar of molasses, "this is a very interesting situation." I poured molasses. "So many things could happen. For instance, Lon Cohen isn't the only one at the *Gazette* who knows I was after pictures of Mr. and Mrs. Bynoe on Wednesday. For instance, when Cramer learns that the film has been removed from my camera—*your* camera—he'll probably send a squad with a search warrant. For in—"

"I'm eating," Wolfe muttered peevishly.

"But I'm not discussing business. This isn't business, this is just a cliff you tumbled over while in pursuit of pleasure, and you're hanging by your fingernails. So am I. For instance, if they find the driver of the taxi, and they will if they decide to, they'll learn that Tabby had company and that we came here. If I had known then that there had been a murder he wouldn't have brought us here, but I didn't. For in—"

"Get rid of the film," Wolfe ordered.

"Right. First thing in the morning. But that's a good camera, and if the needle was shot at her the way Cramer thinks it was, and if I happened to press the button while the needle was going by, it might show. I know a place that will develop that kind of film in short order for a price. How about it?"

Wolfe said yes.

"Okay. Again for instance, if Cramer does send a squad with a warrant when he finds the camera empty, and he might, what about the orchids? If you can't bear to ditch them, I suggest hiding them in the plant rooms among a lot of foliage. Of course that wouldn't work if Bynoe was along, but that's not very—"

The phone rang. I got up and went to the kitchen extension on a shelf, and got it.

"Nero Wolfe's residence, Archie Goodwin speaking."

An educated male voice, low and even, said that it wished to speak with Mr. Wolfe, please, and I asked for its name, please, and it said it preferred not to give its name on the phone, and that made it a problem. But after I had explained that Mr. Wolfe was at the dinner table and not to be disturbed, and I was his confidential assistant, and I wasn't permitted to make an appointment without a name, he decided to come clean.

The rest was easy. I hung up and returned to my biscuits and molasses, and told Wolfe, "That makes it even more interesting. Excuse me for not checking with you, but I was sure you would want to see him. Mr. Millard Bynoe will be here in half an hour."

IV

Millard Bynoe sat on the red leather chair, but not in it. He had probably never lolled once in all his fifty-five years; and now he sat straight with his fanny only halfway back on the seat, his feet neatly together, and his fists resting on his thighs. "Fists" may give a wrong impression. For a man who has spent his whole life giving away an inherited pile in big chunks, it's only natural to keep his fingers curled tight.

Like everybody else, I was of course familiar with the wide mouth and big ears of Millard Bynoe, but the man he had brought with him, whom he had introduced as Mr. Henry Frimm, was a comparative stranger. I had seen him once before as he had left the church beside Mrs. Bynoe. He was a lot younger than Bynoe and a lot better looking, and he wasn't afraid to unbend. On the yellow chair I had placed for him near the corner of Wolfe's desk, he leaned back and even crossed his legs.

Bynoe had trouble getting started. He told Wolfe twice that he had come to consult him on a delicate matter, and apparently the idea of such a thing was too much for him. He sat through a long moment and then tried again.

"I should explain, Mr. Wolfe, that I have come to you in this emergency because I have full confidence in your ability, your discretion, and your integrity. My friend Lewis Hewitt has often spoken to me of a service you performed for him some years ago, and of your talents and character, and he is a good judge of men. He has also spoken of Mr. Goodwin. So when I learned from the police that Mr. Goodwin was there

87

today, in front of the church, and when I found myself confronted by a delicate problem, I decided to bring it to you."

He stopped. Delicate again. Wolfe prompted him. "And the problem?"

"It is highly confidential. I must rely on your discretion."

"Short of complicity in crime, you may." Wolfe's eyes, steady at him, were half closed. "And if the problem is connected with the death of your wife, I may save time by saying that I am fairly well informed. I know how she was killed. Inspector Cramer has been here to question Mr. Goodwin, and Mr. Goodwin has told me what happened in front of the church. Accept my condolence."

"Thank you." Bynoe tilted his head and straightened it again. "You will understand that I am controlling myself with some difficulty. Then you know about the needle?"

"Yes."

"Do you know that the police assume that it was shot at her from a camera?"

"Yes. Do you challenge that?"

"By no means. I suggested that idea to the police, and found that they were already considering it. I see no other possible explanation. I was beside her in the church, and as we left the church, and every moment until she—" He stopped and his jaw stiffened. After a little it came loose and he went on, "You will excuse me. Until she was overcome. So was Mr. Frimm, and we are positive that no one touched her. In front of the church a man was apparently trying to, but he didn't succeed. Mr. Frimm warded him off. Immediately after that she made a sudden movement and caught her lip with her teeth, and we asked her if something had happened, but she shook her head." His jaw worked. "My wife would not want to make a scene in public. I fully accept the police theory, though my problem arises from it." His head turned. "Henry, I prefer that you explain it. If you will?"

"Of course, Mr. Bynoe, if you wish." Frimm was not enthusiastic. Looking at Wolfe, he cleared his throat. "You probably don't know who I am, or what I am. I am the executive secretary of the Bynoe Rehabilitation Fund, one of Mr. Bynoe's major interests. It was also one of Mrs. Bynoe's major interests; she was quite active in the Fund's work. But that is only to tell you who I am; what Mr. Bynoe wants me to explain is the unfortunate circumstance that I am acquainted with one of the persons with a camera in front of the church. A young woman named Iris Innes."

His eyes went to Bynoe, but Bynoe merely said, "Go ahead, Henry," and Frimm returned to Wolfe.

"In fact, Miss Innes and I were engaged to be married, and it was broken off only a month ago. The police have learned that fact and have questioned me about it. They have also questioned me about my relations with Mrs. Bynoe, and some of their questions indicate a suspicion that my engagement with Miss Innes was broken off on account of my feelings about Mrs. Bynoe—a suspicion that is utterly without foundation. But from their questions it appeared that they were actually considering the possibility that Miss Innes had sufficient reason to want to—uh—to harm Mrs. Bynoe. It was absolutely ridiculous, but I felt it was necessary—more than that, it was my duty—to tell Mr. Bynoe about it."

He looked at Bynoe again, but the philanthropist had his eyes on Wolfe. Frimm asked, "Will that do, Mr. Bynoe?"

Bynoe, not answering, said to Wolfe, "You can see why I said it is a delicate problem. I have spoken with the Police Commissioner, and he was most considerate, but newspaper reporters have already tried to question Frimm about it and the danger is very great. If my wife was murdered it is of course impossible to prevent publicity about a murder, but I will not have her memory defiled by a slur on her personal character—her—her purity. I have also consulted my lawyer, and he has spoken with the District Attorney, but beyond that he seems to think that nothing can be done. So I decided to come to you. If you are as efficient and resourceful as my friend Lewis Hewitt thinks you are, you will know what to do."

Wolfe was frowning at him. "If you hope, Mr. Bynoe, to keep innuendoes out of the newspapers, abandon the idea. Short of that, what do you want?"

"I want my wife's memory kept clear of any taint. I want the police to understand that their suspicion of Miss Innes, of her having a motive to harm my wife, is baseless and unwarranted. If my wife was killed by a poisoned needle shot by one of those people with a camera, and I accept that theory because I don't see how else it could have happened, it must have been one of the three men, and I want him found and punished. Another reason why I came to you is that Mr. Goodwin was there. I understand that he was right next to Miss Innes, between her and one of the men, and surely he can say that her camera was merely an ordinary camera. I want you to stop these absurd and vicious speculations." He uncurled his fists to intertwine his fingers. "My wife was a pure and fine woman, and this cannot be tolerated."

Wolfe nodded. "That's a natural attitude for a man in your position. You have had very little to tolerate. But speculations about a murder can be stopped only one way: expose the culprit." His head turned. "Mr. Frimm. The most obvious question: has Miss Innes a plausible excuse for being there with a camera?"

Frimm nodded. "Oh, yes. More than plausible. She is a professional photographer, on the staff of *Señorita*, the magazine. I haven't spoken with her since—I haven't seen her, but I presume she was on assignment."

"When did you see her last?"

"A month ago. When our engagement was broken off."

"Who and what broke it off?"

"We did. By mutual consent. We agreed that we were not suited for each other." Frimm's lips tightened. "As I told you, Mr. Wolfe, this suspicion of the police is completely ridiculous."

"No doubt." Wolfe went to Bynoe. "You understand, sir, that I cannot undertake to establish negatives. I cannot end the speculations and innuendoes by proving that Mr. Frimm did not discard Miss Innes because Mrs. Bynoe had supplanted her in his desires, and that Miss Innes was not moved to avenge her smart. These facts can be established only by eliminating them; they can be eliminated only by providing a substitute; and the only acceptable substitute is one of the three men who were there with cameras. Do you know anything about them?"

"No. I have been told their names, but I don't remember them. My mind is not working. Henry?"

"Yes, Mr. Bynoe. Joseph Herrick, a newspaper photographer, on the *Gazette*. Augustus Pizzi, with a firm of commercial photographers—just a moment—" Frimm closed his eyes. He opened them. "Yes. All-over Pictures, Incorporated. And Alan Geiss, a free-lance photographer." He saw I was writing in my notebook, and asked if I had them, and I told him yes. He returned to Wolfe. "I had never heard of any of them, and neither had Mr. Bynoe. So far as we know, none of them ever had anything to do with Mrs. Bynoe or with anything she was connected with."

Wolfe grunted. "He wouldn't have, since that would point him. More likely, he was paid to do it; and if he won't talk, as he surely won't, where do we look for the man or woman who paid him? Have you any idea, Mr. Frimm?"

"No, I haven't."

"No faintest notion?"

"No. I don't know of anyone who even disliked Mrs. Bynoe, let alone anyone who might want—who might want her to die."

"Have you, Mr. Bynoe?"

"No. Naturally the police wanted to know that, and I have thought about it. In fact, they insisted, but I could give them no names."

"Then it's no wonder they find Miss Innes attractive." Wolfe lifted his chin. "Let us avoid misunderstanding, sir. If you hire me to end speculations about your wife I will undertake it conditionally, the condition being that I find no reason to doubt your statement that they are without foundation. Should I find such a reason, I withdraw and bill you for my fee, and

91

if I have acquired evidence of a crime I inform the police."

"You will find no such reason," Bynoe said stiffly. "And I assure you I would not expect you to suppress evidence of a crime. Your intimation that I might is offensive." He swallowed. "Mr. Hewitt told me that you would be offensive, and I suppose I must tolerate it—either that or just . . . go home and sit and wait and do nothing." His jaw worked. "I accept your condition. My only alternative— No. I accept it. Do you wish a check for a retainer?"

Wolfe said that wasn't necessary and started asking questions. I had my notebook open, but after half an hour there wasn't much in it but an assortment of negatives. They knew nothing at all about Herrick or Pizzi or Geiss; they could name no one who might have had a motive; Mrs. Bynoe had come from an old and respected family, the daughter of an Episcopalian bishop, and to their knowledge there was no scar on her past; and so on down the line. The only faint glimmer was contributed by Bynoe: that on Friday evening he had thought something was troubling her and had asked her what it was, and she had said that Good Friday was no day to speak of human failings and she wouldn't bother him with it until after Easter. That wasn't much help, since he couldn't furnish a guess on what it had been.

When I went to let them out I stood on the sill long enough to see that the limousine waiting for them at the curb was a Rolls-Royce, and then returned to the office. Wolfe was hunched forward in his chair with his eyes closed and his lips screwed up.

"Does it hurt?" I asked cheerfully.

He grunted.

I stood and looked down at him. "A very fine client," I declared. "He probably has a couple of hundred million left *and* that pink Vanda plant. It's too bad you can't fill his order. The way it stacks up, your best move is to hide the orchids. If only we could figure a way to frame Tabby—"

"Shut up," he growled. His eyes opened. "That

woman. I'll have to see her." He glanced up at the wall clock. "Tonight if possible. Get her here."

"Sure. In a box. She's probably downtown with the DA, if they like her as much as Frimm thinks they do, but you need her worse than they do. I'll whistle her out. First I'll see if she's listed." I went to my desk for the Manhattan phone book, turned to the I's and found an entry: "Innes Iris 116 Arbor . . . . . . SU1vn 7-6608." I told Wolfe, "This must be her," and reached for the phone.

"One moment," he said. "I have a suggestion."

V

At midnight of that Easter Sunday I was propped against the wall of a corridor on an upper floor of 155 Leonard Street, and getting tired of it, having been there well over an hour. After Wolfe had made his suggestion, and I had dialed the Sullivan number and got no answer, I had rung the *Gazette*. Lon Cohen wasn't there, but his assistant told me that the latest report was that Iris Innes was still at the DA's office, and, knowing that they rarely keep at a woman all night even when she is charged, I had got the sedan from the garage, and driven downtown and posted myself outside the anteroom. At midnight I was still posted. Three minutes later she showed. The door opened and there she was, but not alone.

It took me two seconds to size up her escort. He was not an assistant DA. He was not her lawyer. He was therefore a dick on the DA's staff, one I didn't know, and he did not have her in custody. His mission was merely to see her to a police car for transportation. With that settled, I fronted them as they started down the corridor and said, "Hi, Iris. I'll take you home."

"Who are you?" the dick demanded.

"A friend of hers. Any objection?"

"I can use a friend," she said, and took my arm, and we headed for the elevator. The dick said something to our backs, and we ignored it. When we reached the elevator and I glanced back, he was standing there making up his mind whether action was called for, and he was still there when the door opened and I ushered her in. Down in the ground-floor corri-

94

dor a journalist tried to head us off, and, recognizing me as well as her, tagged along out to the sidewalk, where I got rude and gave him an elbow in the ribs.

When we were half a block away I spoke. "I've got a car parked around the corner."

"No, thanks," she said. "Just find me a taxi. I've never been put in a taxi by a prince of the blood. Only you're more like a Boy Scout."

We turned the corner. "Why I took your cue," she said, "he was going to take me home and I had had all I could stand of cops for one day. How did you know I wasn't under arrest?"

"The look on his face. I'm an expert on cops' faces. Also the way he walked." I touched her arm to stop her. "Here's my car." I pulled the door open. "Climb in. You know who I am, and you know I want to say something, or what was I there for? I'll say it on the way to one-sixteen Arbor Street."

She gave me a look. In the dim street light her face was more like the one I had seen twelve hours earlier peering down at me from her perch on the box, not as shadowed and saggy as it had been in the corridor. Apparently I passed, for she turned and got in, and I went around to the other side, ducked in behind the wheel, started the engine, and rolled.

She spoke. "You wanted to say something."

"Yeah. You may know I work for Nero Wolfe."

"Of course."

"Millard Bynoe and Henry Frimm came to see him this evening."

Her head jerked around. "What for?"

"It was confidential. But do you happen to know that you were going to marry Frimm and now you're out?"

"Oh my Lord, here we go again. Let me out. If I can't find a taxi I'll walk."

"I merely ask if you know it."

"Certainly I know it."

"Then I can admit that that entered into the conversation." I took time out to make a left turn. "I presume you also know that the cops think a poisoned needle was shot at Mrs. Bynoe by one of us there with cameras. Or have they saved that for tomorrow?"

"They have not. They have my camera. They showed me the needle."

"Then you're caught up and I can speak my piece. It is widely known that I am a sharp observer, and I have good eyes. If I go to the DA's office to answer questions, say tomorrow morning, and if I say I got a good look at your camera at close range, and I am positive that it had no trick gadgets on it, that may not make them cross you off, but it will certainly cool them down. Especially if I add that I will swear to it on a witness stand. Of course at present it's just an if. What I want to suggest is this, that we go and talk it over with Nero Wolfe. Now."

Her face was turned to me, and, stopping for a red light, I turned mine to her.

"I don't get it," she said.

"It's simple enough. If they suspect that you shot that needle—"

"Oh, I get that. It's you I don't get, and Nero Wolfe." She shut her eyes tight. "I'm too tired to think. It wasn't Henry Frimm that got you—not Henry—and why would Millard Bynoe? Take me home."

My eyes had left her because the light had changed and we were moving. "Mr. Wolfe will explain," I assured her. "When you've had something to eat and drink you'll feel better. He'll tell you what—"

"No! I'm going home!" Her voice was up. "I'll get out at the next light!"

She would have. It was no go. We would have a red light in twenty seconds, and that wasn't time enough to talk her around, and if I pulled over and stopped she would hop out, and if I tried holding her she would yell. Her nerves had had all they could take. "Okay," I told her, "skip it. Home it is. I'll ring you in the morning."

Arbor Street, in the Village, was only three minutes away, and at that time of night on Easter Sunday there was no competition. When I pulled up at the curb in front of 116 she had the door open and was out the instant I stopped, but then she stuck her head back in and was smiling at me, or thought she was. It wasn't much of a smile, but she tried. "Thank you anyway," she said. "I'll sleep on it, if I can sleep."

I waited until she was inside, then headed uptown, drove to the garage and left the car, walked around the corner to the brownstone, and mounted the stoop, but when I used my key on the door it opened only to a two-inch gap. The chain-bolt was on. I pushed the button, and when I had to wait a full minute I knew it would be not Fritz but Wolfe. The bolt clanked and the door swung open and I entered.

"No?" he said in a tone of relief. Of course that was to be expected. I will not say that he would rather be arrested for flower-stealing than tackle a woman, but he was relieved. Postpone the evil hour.

"I got her," I said, taking off my coat, "and I had her in the car. But she balked, and even if I had got her here she would have cracked, so I took her home. I'll try her in the morning. Anything new?"

"No."

"Has Tabby stirred?"

"No. I wish I had never heard of orchids."

I gawked. "You *are* in pain. The worst we can get is thirty days, and they might even let Fritz bring us things." He was pushing the button to open his elevator door. "If they take away our licenses we can peddle orchids," I said to cheer him up, and went to the office to lock the safe.

VI

Monday morning I wasn't at home when the invitation came, by phone, for me to call at the DA's office. At eight-fifteen, after breakfasting in the kitchen as usual, and dialing Iris Innes' number and getting no answer, and going up to Wolfe's room, accompanied by Fritz with Wolfe's breakfast tray, to get instructions, and mounting another flight to tell Tabby good morning and finding him still in bed, I went down to the office, got the roll of film from the drawer, and left the house for a morning walk. Finding it cloudy and windy and raw, I buttoned my topcoat.

Surequick Pix, on Fortieth Street near Lexington, was supposed to be open at nine o'clock, but the door was locked and I had to wait. When the guy came he apparently resented me for finding him late, so I apologized and he promised to have the transparencies ready by five o'clock. That was the best I could get. I left the film, went and found a phone booth, rang Iris Innes, again got no answer, and dialed the number I knew best.

In a moment Wolfe's voice, grumpy as always when he is disturbed in the plant rooms, was in my ear. "Yes?"

"I can get the pictures at five o'clock. No answer at Iris Innes' number. I told Fritz to keep an eye and an ear on Tabby. Do I proceed?"

"No. You are wanted at the District Attorney's office and I suppose you'll have to go."

"I could have forgotten to phone in."

"No. Go. You might learn something." He hung up.

From there on that day was one long dismal fizzle. No working detective ever detected less in nine straight hours than I did that Monday. The first two were spent in going down to Leonard Street for an extended talk with a dick and an assistant DA, which satisfied nobody. When I refused to furnish any biographical details except those connected with the proceedings in front of Saint Thomas's they thought they would charge me as a material witness, but since that would accomplish nothing beyond putting me to the trouble and expense of getting bail, and might possibly mean future trouble for them, they skipped it. The main ruckus was about the film. I admitted that I had removed it from the camera before surrendering the camera to Cramer. They claimed that the film was evidence and I was withholding it. I claimed that while the camera might conceivably be evidence, since they were assuming that the murder weapon had been shot from a camera, the film was absolutely out of it, and it was my property, and if they tried taking it with a writ I knew a lawyer. I conceded that if, when the film was developed, anything showed that might be evidence, as for instance a needle in flight, it would be my duty to produce it. Finally the assistant DA, fed up, told me to beat it but keep myself available, and when I said I would be moving around on errands he instructed me to ring him at least once an hour.

Those errands. Still no answer from Iris Innes' phone, and when I went to Arbor Street no answer to her doorbell either. At the *Gazette* Lon Cohen told me that Joe Herrick was at the DA's office and might be there all day. So was Iris Innes, but he wasn't sure about Alan Geiss and Augustus Pizzi. After thirty minutes out for lunch at an oyster bar I called on All-over Pictures, Inc., but no one there was answering questions about Augustus Pizzi. Having got the address of Alan Geiss, the free-lance, from Lon Cohen, I took the subway to Washington Heights to pass the time, and time was what I passed. His landlady, getting a kick out of it, one of her lodgers having his picture in the paper, would have loved to talk, but she was cross-eyed and I was cross, so I left her, went and found a phone booth and made my three hourly calls: to Iris Innes, no answer; to Wolfe, no news; and to the assistant DA, whose name was Doyle. When Doyle said he wanted to see me I was just as well pleased. Debating with him about the nature of evidence would be fully as helpful as what I was doing and would be more fun. I sought the subway.

But Doyle didn't resume the discussion of evidence. As soon as I was seated at the end of his desk he took an object from a drawer and handed it to me and asked, "Do you know that man?"

It was an unusually good police picture, an excellent likeness, both the front view and the profile, but I thought it proper to study it a little. Having done so, I nodded and dropped it on the desk.

"I wouldn't swear to it, but it looks like a specimen I met once in connection with a case—wait and I'll tell you his name. Yeah. Tabby. A couple of years ago. I could have handed him in for a little mistake he made but didn't. Why, has he made another mistake?"

"He has been identified as the man who grabbed the orchids off of Mrs. Bynoe as she lay on the sidewalk. By three people."

"I'll be darned. He has, or the picture has?"

"The picture—when did you see him last?"

I grinned at him. "Now look. I told you this morning what Mr. Wolfe told Inspector Cramer. Cramer himself said that he couldn't have stuck the needle in her when he took the orchids because she was already dying, so what has it got to do with the murder? It's like the film, exactly. I realize we're not in a courtroom, so you're not bound by the rules of evidence, but I am. I don't intend—"

"When did you see him last?"

"Nope. Connect him up. Make it material and I'll tell you every word I ever exchanged with him. I have a wonderful memory."

He was unquestionably displeased. It looked for a while as if the next time I touched a sidewalk I would be under bond, and when he left the room, telling me to wait, with a dick there for company, I was sure of it, but when he came back after a long quarter of an hour he had something else on his mind and merely told me that was all. He didn't even warn me to keep myself available.

So I got back uptown and to the office of Sure-quick Pix shortly after five o'clock, only to find I was in for another wait. My job wasn't finished and wouldn't be for an hour. He explained that the day after Easter was one of the busiest days of the year, and I went out to a booth and phoned Wolfe and tried Iris Innes again, and bought evening papers to get the latest on the Bynoe murder. There were pictures of all the church-front photographers. The one of me was a shot taken that day at the *Gazette* office, and I was squinting, which makes me look older.

A little after six the transparencies were ready, and, while I didn't expect to find that I had caught anything as interesting as a needle in the air, there was a viewer right there on the counter and I thought I might as well take a look. There were eleven of them altogether. Five were close-ups I had taken previously up in the plant rooms, two were of the exodus from the church before Mrs. Bynoe appeared, and four showed her and her escorts as they approached. The one I looked at longest was the fourth and last, and it confirmed my memory of what I had seen in the finder: all it had of Tabby was his arm and shoulder and the back of his head, and he was a good three feet away from Mrs. Bynoe.

No needle, no murder evidence, but a little caution wouldn't hurt, so I asked the man for another envelope, which he kindly provided with no extra charge, put the Bynoe pictures in it, and put one envelope in my right-hand pocket and the other in my left. If the Mayor or the Governor or J. Edgar Hoover stopped me on the sidewalk and asked to see the pictures I took of the Easter parade it wasn't necessary for him to know that I had concentrated on Mrs. Millard Bynoe. No one stopped me. It was half past six, still daylight, as I mounted the stoop of the brownstone, used my key, and found, to my surprise, that the chain-bolt wasn't on.

But that surprise was nothing to what followed.

The big old oak rack was so covered with hats and coats that I had to put mine on a chair, and Wolfe's voice, raised a little for an audience, was coming through the open door to the office. I walked the length of the hall, looked in, saw District Attorney Skinner seated at my desk in my chair, and the room full of people. It was a shock. I don't like other people sitting in my chair, not even a District Attorney.

VII

As I entered, heads turned and Wolfe stopped talking. Since my chair was occupied I wanted to ask him if I was invited, but held it; and as I circled around the cluster of chairs he spoke.

"That's Mr. Goodwin's desk, Mr. Skinner. If you don't mind?"

That helped a little, but not much. He had never before arranged to stage a charade without even telling me, and besides, I had spent a good part of the day, under instructions, trying to corral four of those present: Iris Innes and Joe Herrick, whom I was acquainted with, and Alan Geiss and Augustus Pizzi, whom I had seen standing on boxes the day before. There was a vacant chair back of Geiss, and Skinner got up and moved to it. Inspector Cramer was just beyond, and in front of him was Henry Frimm. In the red leather chair, exactly as he had sat the previous evening, using only half the seat, with his back straight and his fists on his thighs, was Millard Bynoe.

Bynoe and Frimm and Cramer and Skinner I could stand, but the sight of the four photographers, after the day I had spent, was too much for me. I stood at my desk and asked Wolfe, "Am I in the way?"

"Sit down, Archie." He was brusque. "The idea of this gathering came from Mr. Bynoe, and he arranged for it with Mr. Skinner. We have been at it half an hour but have made no progress. Sit down."

I accepted that, since a billionaire philanthropist might plausibly have considerable drag with a District Attorney, but even so, if they had been there by six

103

o'clock the preparations must have taken more than an hour, and I had phoned in at a quarter past five and he hadn't mentioned it. He needed a lesson in co-operation. I got the envelope from my right-hand pocket and tossed it on his desk. If Cramer got curious and demanded a look, and wondered why I had been specifically interested in Mrs. Bynoe, let Wolfe juggle it. Of course, he would merely pick it up and drop it in a drawer.

But he didn't. The Centrex had been bought for making a permanent record of color variations in blos-soms, and the viewer was there on the desk. He pulled it to him, took the transparencies from the envelope, inserted one, inspected it, removed it, and inserted an-other.

Cramer spoke up. "What have you got there?"

"I beg your indulgence," Wolfe muttered, and went on inspecting, shifting from one to another. He seemed to have a favorite, and I guessed it was the last of the series. After he had inserted it a third time and given it a good long minute, he lifted his head.

"Mr. Cramer and Mr. Skinner." His voice had an edge. "If you will please come and take a look? This is one of the pictures Mr. Goodwin took yester-day—the last one."

He turned the viewer around and pushed it across the desk. Cramer, there first, bent over to get his eyes at the right level. After ten seconds he grunted and moved aside to give Skinner a chance. The DA took a little longer, then straightened up.

"Interesting," he told Wolfe. "He was certainly focused on Mrs. Bynoe. That man in front, apparently reaching for her—did he reach her?"

"I think not. Mr. Goodwin says he didn't, and I gather that the others agree. But there is, to my eye, a suggestive detail. I wish you gentlemen would look again. Closely."

They did so, longer than before. When they had finished Cramer demanded, "What's the detail?"

Wolfe pulled the viewer back to him and took another look, then raised his head. "I may be wrong,"

104

he conceded, "But it deserves inquiry and I would like to test it. Not with you gentlemen, for you have seen the picture. So has Mr. Goodwin. And Mr. Bynoe and Mr. Frimm were there." His eyes moved. "Miss Innes and Mr. Herrick, if you will oblige us? Miss Innes, you will rise and move back a little so we can all see. You are Mrs. Bynoe, crossing the sidewalk and facing the cameras. Archie, you are the man who was apparently trying to reach her. Get in front of her, at the proper distance, with your back to the cameras. Mr. Herrick, you are Mrs. Bynoe's escort, the one at her left. Take your position. No, closer to her, quite close, according to the picture. That's better. Now. As you are crossing the sidewalk beside her, moving slowly, a man is suddenly there, facing her, apparently intending to touch her. Instinctively and abruptly you stretch your arms in front of her to fend him off. Don't think about it; just do it; it was actually a reflex. Go ahead!"

I, in Tabby's position, jerked forward an inch, and Herrick stuck his arms out in front of Iris Innes.

"Again, please," Wolfe commanded. "You're not attacking him; you are merely barring him off. Again!"

I jerked again and Herrick flung his arms across. Wolfe nodded. "Thank you. Miss Innes, keep your position. Mr. Pizzi, will you demonstrate for us?"

Skinner said something to Cramer that I didn't catch as Augustus Pizzi, who was barrel-shaped with slick black hair, replaced Joe Herrick and put himself in the mood by glaring at me. He performed with more zip than Herrick, and, after he had repeated it twice on request, made way for Alan Geiss. Geiss, from the expression on his long bony face, thought it was a lot of hooey, but he went through with it, twice.

"That will do," Wolfe told us. "If you will resume your seats?" He turned the viewer around and pushed it across the desk. "Mr. Bynoe and Mr. Frimm, I think you should have a look at the picture."

They had to wait because both Cramer and Skinner were at it ahead of them, for another go. Millard

Bynoe was last. He peered at it for three seconds, not more, and then returned to the red leather chair and got his spine straight.

Cramer rasped, "I see where you're headed, Wolfe, but watch your step."

"I shall," Wolfe assured him. His eyes went from right to left and back again. "Of course I am going to explore the possibility that Henry Frimm killed Mrs. Bynoe. After that demonstration it would be witless not to. All three of the demonstrators held their arms in approximately the same position, with their palms outward, whereas in the picture Mr. Frimm's right arm is turned so that the palm is inward; and moreover, the tips of his thumb and forefinger are touching, which is absurd. All the demonstrators had their fingers spread on both hands. The position of Mr. Frimm's hand and fingers is explicable under one assumption: that he was about to stick a needle into Mrs. Bynoe."

I was aware that Skinner said something, and that Frimm started to leave his chair and decided not to, and that Iris Innes made a noise, but only vaguely because of Millard Bynoe. His jaw had dropped open and his head was moving from side to side, from Wolfe to Frimm and back again, a perfect picture of a goof. He was making no effort to speak.

Frimm did make an effort. "This is before witnesses, Wolfe."

Wolfe eyed him. "Yes, sir, I know. I have seen that picture only now, but I was too pressed for prudence. Mr. Bynoe was so urgent about the job he hired me to do that I permitted him to get all these people here, though I hadn't the slightest idea what I would do with them, and probably nothing would have been accomplished if Mr. Goodwin hadn't turned up with that picture. You know what Mr. Bynoe hired me for; do you challenge my right to explore a possibility?"

"No, I don't challenge you." Frimm swallowed. "But there are witnesses."

"There are indeed." Wolfe's eyes were half closed. "There is no question about opportunity; you were there, and your hand was there. The point arises:

106

why did you select so public an arena, with cameras pointed at you? Obviously you did so deliberately, calculating that it would be assumed that the needle was shot from one of the cameras, as indeed it has been. Two questions remain: where did you get the needle and the poison? and why did you do it?"

He turned a hand over. "The first is for Mr. Cramer and his army. His talents and resources are ideally fitted for that. For the second, I can at the moment only offer suggestions. We are exploring possibilities, and one is offered by the fact that you are the operating head of the Bynoe Rehabilitation Fund and Mrs. Bynoe was active in its affairs. She may have discovered, or suspected, that you were making free with the Fund's money, and was going to tell her husband. That can be explored by an examination of the Fund's books. Another suggestion is offered by Mr. Bynoe's high regard for his wife's integrity—he prefers the word 'purity.' It might be that—"

Bynoe put in. He had his jaw back under control and had found his voice. It had changed, though; it came out harsh and louder than necessary. "You will omit that, Mr. Wolfe."

"No, sir," Wolfe declared, "I will not." He kept his eyes at Frimm. "It might be that you had a try at her integrity and were repulsed. Assuredly you would not have killed her because she indulged you, but what if she refused to? And what if you were so persistent that she resolved to inform her husband? You would have lost your job and all that it meant to you. Of course, an exploration of this possibility may be extremely difficult. If you have peculated there are records that will reveal it, but a rebuffed gallantry may have left no record. There may be no one alive, except you, who knows anything about it. In that case—"

"I do."

All eyes went to Iris Innes. Hers were aimed at Frimm, and he twisted around to meet them.

"You tinhorn Casanova," she said in a voice that wanted to shake but she wouldn't let it. "Hinting to me that you had her, and I knew all the time you didn't. That was what finally gave me sense enough to

107

realize what you were. Remember, Hank? Remember what you told me? I've kept it to myself because I was having enough trouble already, but now they can have it." Her eyes went to Wolfe. "Yes, I know about it. He told me—"

Frimm dived at her. I was too far away, and so was Cramer. Skinner was close enough, but DA's are for thinking, not acting. It was Joe Herrick who stopped him. Frimm did get his hands on her, at least he reached her, but Herrick grabbed his arm and whirled him around, and then Cramer and I were both there, and if you can believe it, Millard Bynoe was there with us. I actually think he was going to use a fist at last, after all the years, but Cramer got in between them and I pushed Frimm down onto a chair. Also I had his arms pinned, since another possibility to be explored was that he had another needle.

Bynoe, his tight fists hanging, faced Cramer and spoke. "The needle shot from a camera—he suggested that. He suggested it to me, and I suggested it to you." He was having trouble with his jaw. "And my wife had decided not to tell me on Good Friday. She was waiting until after Easter. He knew that. Of course he knew. He—" His jaw suddenly clamped and he swung around to Frimm.

"Take it easy, Mr. Bynoe." Cramer had a hand on his shoulder.

Wolfe growled, "Will somebody get Miss Innes up and onto a chair?"

VIII

But rebuffed gallantry was never mentioned at the trial, and Iris Innes wasn't called. It wasn't necessary, since they could show that Frimm had made free with the exchequer of the Bynoe Rehabilitation Fund to the tune of more than a quarter of a million, and since Cramer justified Wolfe's rating of his talents and resources by discovering how and where he had got the needle and the poison.

If you would like to see the plant of flamingo-pink Vanda, ring me and if I'm not too busy I'll arrange it. It has a spot all to itself on a bench up in the plant rooms. It came in addition to Bynoe's check in payment of Wolfe's bill for services rendered. I have no proof that Wolfe dropped any hints to Bynoe about the Vanda, but I wasn't with him when he visited Bynoe's greenhouses, and I am entitled to my opinion.

And if you have some little confidential chore you would like to hire Tabby for, I might be able to put you in touch with him, but I warn you not to offer him too much. It goes to his head.

Fourth of July Picnic

I

Flora Korby swiveled her head, with no hat hiding any of her dark brown hair, to face me with her dark brown eyes. She spoke.

"I guess I should have brought my car and led the way."

"I'm doing fine," I assured her. "I could shut one eye too."

"Please don't," she begged. "I'm stupefied as it is. May I have your autograph—I mean when we stop?"

Since she was highly presentable I didn't mind her assuming that I was driving with one hand because my right arm wanted to stretch across her shoulders, though she was wrong. I had left the cradle long ago. But there was no point in explaining to her that Nero Wolfe, who was in the back seat, had a deep distrust of moving vehicles and hated to ride in one unless I drove it, and therefore I was glad to have an excuse to drive with one hand because that would make it more thrilling for him.

Anyway, she might have guessed it. The only outside interest that Wolfe permits to interfere with his personal routine of comfort, not to mention luxury, is Rusterman's restaurant. Its founder, Marko Vukcic, was Wolfe's oldest and closest friend; and when Vukcic died, leaving the restaurant to members of the staff and making Wolfe executor of his estate, he also left a letter asking Wolfe to see to it that the restaurant's standards and reputation were maintained; and Wolfe had done so, making unannounced visits there once or twice a week, and sometimes even oftener, without ever grumbling—well, hardly ever. But he sure did grumble when Felix, the maître d'hôtel, asked him to make a speech at the Independence Day picnic of the United Restaurant Workers of America. Hereafter I'll make it URWA.

He not only grumbled, he refused. But Felix kept after him, and Wolfe finally gave in when Felix came to the office one day with reinforcements: Paul Rago, the sauce chef at the Churchill; James Korby, the president of URWA; H. L. Griffin, a food and wine importer who supplied hard-to-get items not only for Rusterman's but also for Wolfe's own table; and Philip Holt, URWA's director of organization. They also were to be on the program at the picnic, and their main appeal was that they simply had to have the man who was responsible for keeping Rusterman's the best restaurant in New York after the death of Marko Vukcic. Since Wolfe is only as vain as three peacocks, and since he had loved Marko if he ever loved anyone, that got him. There had been another inducement: Philip Holt had agreed to lay off of Fritz, Wolfe's chef and housekeeper. For three years Fritz had been visiting the kitchen at Rusterman's off and on as a consultant, and Holt had been pestering him, insisting that he had to join URWA. You can guess how Wolfe liked that.

Since I do everything that has to be done in connection with Wolfe's business and his rare social activities, except that he thinks he does all the thinking, and we won't go into that now, it would be up to me to get him to the scene of the picnic, Culp's Meadows on Long Island, on the Fourth of July. Around the end of June James Korby phoned and introduced his daughter Flora. She told me that the directions to Culp's Meadows were very complicated, and I said that all directions on Long Island were very complicated, and she said she had better drive us out in her car.

I liked her voice, that is true, but also I have a lot of foresight, and it occurred to me immediately that it would be a new and exciting experience for my employer to watch me drive with one hand, so I told her

114

that, while it must be Wolfe's car and I must drive, I would deeply appreciate it if she would come along and tell me the way. That was how it happened, and that was why, when we finally rolled through the gate at Culp's Meadows, after some thirty miles of Long Island parkways and another ten of grade intersections and trick turns, Wolfe's lips were pressed so tight he didn't have any. He had spoken only once, around the fourth or fifth mile, when I had swept around a slow-poke.

"Archie. You know quite well."

"Yes, sir." Of course I kept my eyes straight ahead. "But it's an impulse, having my arm like this, and I'm afraid to take it away because if I fight an impulse it makes me nervous, and driving when you're nervous is bad."

A glance in the mirror showed me his lips tightening, and they stayed tight.

Passing through the gate at Culp's Meadows, and winding around as directed by Flora Korby, I used both hands. It was a quarter to three, so we were on time, since the speeches were scheduled for three o'clock. Flora was sure a space would have been saved for us back of the tent, and after threading through a few acres of parked cars I found she was right, and rolled to a stop with the radiator only a couple of yards from the canvas. She hopped out and opened the rear door on her side, and I did likewise on mine. Wolfe's eyes went right to her, and then left to me. He was torn. He didn't want to favor a woman, even a young and pretty one, but he absolutely had to show me what he thought of one-handed driving. His eyes went right again, the whole seventh of a ton of him moved, and he climbed out on her side.

II

The tent, on a wooden platform raised three feet above the ground, not much bigger than Wolfe's office, was crowded with people, and I wormed through to the front entrance and on out, where the platform extended into the open air. There was plenty of air, with a breeze dancing in from the direction of the ocean, and plenty of sunshine. A fine day for the Fourth of July. The platform extension was crammed with chairs, most of them empty. I can't report on the condition of the meadow's grass because my view was obstructed by ten thousand restaurant workers and their guests, maybe more. A couple of thousand of them were in a solid mass facing the platform, presumably those who wanted to be up front for the speeches, and the rest were sprayed around all over, clear across to a fringe of trees and a row of sheds.

Flora's voice came from behind my shoulder. "They're coming out, so if there's a chair you like, grab it. Except the six up front; they're for the speakers."

Naturally I started to tell her I wanted the one next to hers, but didn't get it out because people came jostling out of the tent onto the extension. Thinking I had better warn Wolfe that the chair he was about to occupy for an hour or so was about half as wide as his fanny, to give him time to fight his impulses, I worked past to the edge of the entrance, and when the exodus had thinned out I entered the tent. Five men were standing grouped beside a cot which was touching the canvas of the far side, and a man was lying on the cot. To my left Nero Wolfe was bending over to peer

116

at the contents of a metal box there on a table with its lid open. I stepped over for a look and saw a collection of bone-handled knives, eight of them, with blades varying in length from six inches up to twelve. They weren't shiny, but they looked sharp, worn narrow by a lot of use for a lot of years. I asked Wolfe whose throat he was going to cut.

"They are Dubois," he said. "Real old Dubois. The best. They belong to Mr. Korby. He brought them to use in a carving contest, and he won, as he should. I would gladly steal them." He turned. "Why don't they let that man alone?"

I turned too, and through a gap in the group saw that the man on the cot was Philip Holt, URWA's director of organization. "What's the matter with him?" I asked.

"Something he ate. They think snails. Probably the wrong kind of snails. A doctor gave him something to help his bowels handle them. Why don't they leave him alone with his bowels?"

"I'll go ask," I said, and moved.

As I approached the cot James Korby was speaking. "I say he should be taken to a hospital, in spite of what that doctor said. Look at his color!"

Korby, short, pudgy, and bald, looked more like a restaurant customer than a restaurant worker, which may have been one reason he was president of URWA.

"I agree," Dick Vetter said emphatically. I had never seen Dick Vetter in person, but I had seen him often enough on his TV show—in fact, a little too often. If I quit dialing his channel he wouldn't miss me, since twenty million Americans, mostly female, were convinced that he was the youngest and handsomest MC on the waves. Flora Korby had told me he would be there, and why. His father had been a bus boy in a Broadway restaurant for thirty years, and still was because he wouldn't quit.

Paul Rago did not agree, and said so. "It would be a pity," he declared. He made it "peety," his accent having tapered off enough not to make it "peetee." With his broad shoulders and six feet, his slick black

117

hair going gray, and his mustache with pointed tips that was still all black, he looked more like an ambassador from below the border than a sauce chef. He was going on. "He is the most important man in the union—except, of course, the president—and he should make an appearance on the platform. Perhaps he can before we are through."

"I hope you will pardon me." That was H. L. Griffin, the food and wine importer. He was a skinny little runt, with a long narrow chin and something wrong with one eye, but he spoke with the authority of a man whose firm occupied a whole floor in one of the midtown hives. "I may have no right to an opinion, since I am not a member of your great organization, but you have done me the honor of inviting me to take part in your celebration of our country's independence, and I do know of Phil Holt's high standing and wide popularity among your members. I would merely say that I feel that Mr. Rago is right, that they will be disappointed not to see him on the platform. I hope I am not being presumptuous."

From outside the tent, from the loudspeakers at the corners of the platform, a booming voice had been calling to the picnickers scattered over the meadow to close in and prepare to listen. As the group by the cot went on arguing, a state trooper in uniform, who had been standing politely aside, came over and joined them and took a look at Philip Holt, but offered no advice. Wolfe also approached for a look. Myself, I would have said that the place for him was a good bed with an attractive nurse smoothing his brow. I saw him shiver all over at least three times. He decided it himself, finally, by muttering at them to let him alone and turning on his side to face the canvas. Flora Korby had come in, and she put a blanket over him, and I noticed that Dick Vetter made a point of helping her. The breeze was sweeping through and one of them said he shouldn't be in a draft, and Wolfe told me to lower the flap of the rear entrance, and I did so. The flap didn't want to stay down, so I tied the plastic tape fastening to hold it, in a single bowknot. Then they all marched out through the front entrance to the platform, including the state trooper, and I brought up the rear. As Korby passed the table he stopped to lower the lid on the box of knives, real old Dubois.

The speeches lasted an hour and eight minutes, and the ten thousand URWA members and guests took them standing like ladies and gentlemen. You are probably hoping I will report them word for word, but I didn't take them down and I didn't listen hard enough to engrave them on my memory. At that, the eagle didn't scream as much or as loud as I had expected. From my seat in the back row I could see most of the audience, and it was quite a sight.

The first speaker was a stranger, evidently the one who had been calling on them to gather around while we were in the tent, and after a few fitting remarks he introduced James Korby. While Korby was orating, Paul Rago left his seat, passed down the aisle in the center, and entered the tent. Since he had plugged for an appearance by Philip Holt I thought his purpose might be to drag him out alive or dead, but it wasn't. In a minute he was back again, and just in time, for he had just sat down when Korby finished and Rago was introduced.

The faces out front had all been serious for Korby, but Rago's accent through the loudspeakers had most of them grinning by the time he warmed up. When Korby left his chair and started down the aisle I suspected him of walking out on Rago because Rago had walked out on him, but maybe not, since his visit in the tent was even shorter than Rago's had been. He came back out and returned to his chair, and listened attentively to the accent.

Next came H. L. Griffin, the importer, and the chairman had to lower the mike for him. His voice took the loudspeakers better than any of the others, and in fact he was darned good. It was only fair, I thought, to have the runt of the bunch take the cake, and I was all for the cheers from the throng that kept him on his feet a full minute after he finished. He really woke them up, and they were still yelling when he turned and went down the aisle to the tent, and it took the chairman a while to calm them down. Then, just as he started to introduce Dick Vetter, the TV star suddenly bounced up and started down the aisle with a determined look on his face, and it was easy to guess why. He thought Griffin was going to take advantage of the enthusiasm he had aroused by hauling Philip Holt out to the platform, and he was going to stop him. But he didn't have to. He was still two steps short of the tent entrance when Griffin emerged alone. Vetter moved aside to let him pass and then disappeared into the tent. As Griffin proceeded to his chair in the front row there were some scattered cheers from the crowd, and the chairman had to quiet them again before he could go on. Then he introduced Dick Vetter, who came out of the tent and along to the mike, which had to be raised again, at just the right moment.

As Vetter started to speak, Nero Wolfe arose and headed for the tent, and I raised my brows. Surely, I thought, he's not going to involve himself in the Holt problem; and then, seeing the look on his face, I caught on. The edges of the wooden chair seat had been cutting into his fanny for nearly an hour and he was in a tantrum, and he wanted to cool off a little before he was called to the mike. I grinned at him sympathetically as he passed and then gave my ear to Vetter. His soapy voice (I say soapy) came through the loudspeakers in a flow of lather, and after a couple of minutes of it I was thinking that it was only fair for Griffin, the runt, to sound like a man, and for Vetter, the handsome young idol of millions, to sound like whipped cream, when my attention was called. Wolfe was at the tent entrance, crooking a finger at me. As I got up and approached he backed into the tent, and I followed. He crossed to the rear entrance, lifted the flap, maneuvered his bulk through the hole, and held the flap for me. When I had made it he descended the five steps to the ground, walked to the car, grabbed the handle of the rear door, and pulled. Nothing doing. He turned to me.

"Unlock it."

I stood. "Do you want something?"

"Unlock it and get in and get the thing started. We're going."

"We are like hell. You've got a speech to make."

He glared at me. He knows my tones of voice as well as I know his. "Archie," he said, "I am not being eccentric. There is a sound and cogent reason and I'll explain on the way. Unlock this door."

I shook my head. "Not till I hear the reason. I admit it's your car." I took the keys from my pocket and offered them. "Here. I resign."

"Very well." He was grim. "That man on the cot is dead. I lifted the blanket to adjust it. One of those knives is in his back, clear to the handle. He is dead. If we are still here when the discovery is made you know what will happen. We will be here all day, all night, a week, indefinitely. That is intolerable. We can answer questions at home as well as here. Confound it, unlock the door!"

"How dead is he?"

"I have told you he is dead."

"Okay. You ought to know better. You do know better. We're stuck. They wouldn't ask us questions at home, they'd haul us back out here. They'd be waiting for us on the stoop and you wouldn't get inside the house." I returned the keys to my pocket. "Running out when you're next on the program, that would be nice. The only question is do we report it now or do you make your speech and let someone else find it, and you can answer that."

He had stopped glaring. He took in a long, deep breath, and when it was out again he said, "I'll make my speech."

"Fine. It'd be a shame to waste it. A question. Just now when you lifted the flap to come out I didn't see you untie the tape fastening. Was it already untied?"

"Yes."

"That makes it nice." I turned and went to the steps, mounted, raised the flap for him, and followed him into the tent. He crossed to the front and on out, and I stepped to the cot. Philip Holt lay facing the wall, with the blanket up to his neck, and I pulled it down far enough to see the handle of the knife, an inch to the right of the point of the shoulder blade. The knife blade was all buried. I lowered the blanket some more to get at a hand, pinched a fingertip hard for ten seconds, released it, and saw it stay white. I picked some fluff from the blanket and dangled it against his nostrils for half a minute. No movement. I put the blanket back as I had found it, went to the metal box on the table and lifted the lid, and saw that the shortest knife, the one with the six-inch blade, wasn't there.

As I went to the rear entrance and raised the flap, Dick Vetter's lather or whipped cream, whichever you prefer, came to an end through the loudspeakers, and as I descended the five steps the meadowful of picknickers was cheering.

Our sedan was the third car on the right from the foot of the steps. The second car to the left of the steps was a 1955 Plymouth, and I was pleased to see that it still had an occupant, having previously noticed her—a woman with careless gray hair topping a wide face and a square chin, in the front seat but not behind the wheel.

I circled around to her side and spoke through the open window. "I beg your pardon. May I introduce myself?"

"You don't have to, young man. Your name's Archie Goodwin, and you work for Nero Wolfe, the detective." She had tired gray eyes. "You were just out here with him."

"Right. I hope you won't mind if I ask you something. How long have you been sitting here?"

"Long enough. But it's all right, I can hear the speeches. Nero Wolfe is just starting to speak now."

"Have you been here since the speeches started?"

"Yes, I have. I ate too much of the picnic stuff and I didn't feel like standing up in that crowd, so I came to sit in the car."

"Then you've been here all the time since the speeches began?"

"That's what I said. Why do you want to know?"

"I'm just checking on something. If you don't mind. Has anyone gone into the tent or come out of it while you've been here?"

Her tired eyes woke up a little. "Ha," she said,

"so something's missing. I'm not surprised. What's missing?"

"Nothing, as far as I know. I'm just checking a certain fact. Of course you saw Mr. Wolfe and me come out and go back in. Anyone else, either going or coming?"

"You're not fooling me, young man. Something's missing, and you're a detective."

I grinned at her. "All right, have it your way. But I do want to know, if you don't object."

"I don't object. As I told you, I've been right here ever since the speeches started, I got here before that. And nobody has gone into the tent, nobody but you and Nero Wolfe, and I haven't either. I've been right here. If you want to know about me, my name is Anna Banau, Mrs. Alexander Banau, and my husband is a captain at Zoller's—"

A scream came from inside the tent, an all-out scream from a good pair of lungs. I moved, to the steps, up, and past the flap into the tent. Flora Korby was standing near the cot with her back to it, her hand covering her mouth. I was disappointed in her. Granting that a woman has a right to scream when she finds a corpse, she might have kept it down until Wolfe had finished his speech.

III

It was a little after four o'clock when Flora Korby screamed. It was 4:34 when a glance outside through a crack past the flap of the tent's rear entrance, the third such glance I had managed to make, showed me that the Plymouth containing Mrs. Alexander Banau was gone. It was 4:39 when the medical examiner arrived with his bag and found that Philip Holt was still dead. It was 4:48 when the scientists came, with cameras and fingerprint kits and other items of equipment, and Wolfe and I and the others were herded out to the extension, under guard. It was 5:16 when I counted a total of seventeen cops, state and county, in uniform and out, on the job. It was 5:30 when Wolfe muttered at me bitterly that it would certainly be all night. It was 5:52 when a chief of detectives named Baxter got so personal with me that I decided, finally and definitely, not to play. It was 6:21 when we all left Culp's Meadows for an official destination. There were four in our car: one in uniform with Wolfe in the back seat, and one in his own clothes with me in front. Again I had someone beside me to tell me the way, but I didn't put my arm across his shoulders.

There had been some conversing with us separately, but most of it had been a panel discussion, open air, out on the platform extension, so I knew pretty well how things stood. Nobody was accusing anybody. Three of them—Korby, Rago, and Griffin—gave approximately the same reason for their visits to the tent during the speechmaking: that they were concerned about Philip Holt and wanted to see if he was all right. The fourth, Dick Vetter, gave the reason I had guessed, that he thought Griffin might bring Holt out to the platform, and he intended to stop him. Vetter, by the way, was the only one who raised a fuss about being detained. He said that it hadn't been easy to get away from his duties that afternoon, and he had a studio rehearsal scheduled for six o'clock, and he absolutely had to be there. At 6:21, when we all left for the official destination, he was fit to be tied.

None of them claimed to know for sure that Holt had been alive at the time he visited the tent; they all had supposed he had fallen asleep. All except Vetter said they had gone to the cot and looked at him, at his face, and had suspected nothing wrong. None of them had spoken to him. To the question, "Who do you think did it and why?" they all gave the same answer: someone must have entered the tent by the rear entrance, stabbed him, and departed. The fact that the URWA director of organization had got his stomach into trouble and had been attended by a doctor in the tent had been no secret, anything but.

I have been leaving Flora out, since I knew and you know she was clear, but the cops didn't. I overheard one of them tell another one it was probably her, because stabbing a sick man was more like something a woman would do than a man.

Of course the theory that someone had entered by the back door made the fastening of the tent flap an important item. I said I had tied the tape before we left the tent, and they all agreed that they had seen me do so except Dick Vetter, who said he hadn't noticed because he had been helping to arrange the blanket over Holt; and Wolfe and I both testified that the tape was hanging loose when we had entered the tent while Vetter was speaking. Under this theory the point wasn't who had untied it, since the murderer could have easily reached through the crack from the outside and jerked the knot loose; the question was when. On that none of them was any help. All four said they hadn't noticed whether the tape was tied or not when they went inside the tent.

That was how it stood, as far as I knew, when we left Culp's Meadows. The official destination turned out to be a building I had been in before a time or two, not as a murder suspect—a county courthouse back of a smooth green lawn with a couple of big trees. First we were collected in a room on the ground floor, and, after a long wait, were escorted up one flight and through a door that was inscribed DISTRICT ATTORNEY.

At least 91.2 per cent of the district attorneys in the State of New York think they would make fine tenants of the governor's mansion at Albany, and that should be kept in mind in considering the conduct of DA James R. Delaney. To him at least four of that bunch, and possibly all five, were upright, important citizens in positions to influence segments of the electorate. His attitude as he attacked the problem implied that he was merely chairing a meeting of a community council called to deal with a grave and difficult emergency—except, I noticed, when he was looking at or speaking to Wolfe or me. Then his smile quit working, his tone sharpened, and his eyes had a different look.

With a stenographer at a side table taking it down, he spent an hour going over it with us, or rather with them, with scattered contributions from Chief of Detectives Baxter and others who had been at the scene, and then spoke his mind.

"It seems," he said, "to be the consensus that some person unknown entered the tent from the rear, stabbed him, and departed. There is the question, how could such a person have known the knife would be there at hand? but he need not have known. He might have decided to murder only when he saw the knives, or he might have had some other weapon with him, and, seeing the knives, thought one of them would better serve his purpose and used it instead. Either is plausible. It must be admitted that the whole theory is plausible, and none of the facts now known are in contradiction to it. You agree, Chief?"

"Right," Baxter conceded. "Up to now. As long as the known facts are facts."

Delaney nodded. "Certainly. They have to be checked." His eyes took in the audience. "You gentlemen, and you, Miss Korby, you understand that you

126

are to remain in this jurisdiction, the State of New York, until further notice, and you are to be available. With that understood, it seems unnecessary at present to put you under bond as material witnesses. We have your addresses and know where to find you."

He focused on Wolfe, and his tone changed. "With you, Wolfe, the situation is somewhat different. You're a licensed private detective, and so is Goodwin, and the record of your high-handed performances does not inspire confidence in your—uh—candor. There may be some complicated and subtle reasons why the New York City authorities have stood for your tricks, but out here in the suburbs we're more simpleminded. We don't like tricks."

He lowered his chin, which made his eyes slant up under his heavy brows. "Let's see if I've got your story straight. You say that as Vetter started to speak you felt in your pocket for a paper on which you had made notes for your speech, found it wasn't there, thought you had left it in your car, went to get it, and when, after you had entered the tent, it occurred to you that the car was locked and Goodwin had the keys, you summoned him and you and he went out to the car. Then Goodwin remembered that the paper had been left on your desk at your office, and you and he returned to the tent, and you went out to the platform and resumed your seat. Another item: when you went to the rear entrance to leave the tent to go out to the car, the tape fastening of the flap was hanging loose, not tied. Is that your story?"

Wolfe cleared his throat. "Mr. Delaney. I suppose it is pointless to challenge your remark about my candor or to ask you to phrase your question less offensively." His shoulders went up an eighth of an inch, and down. "Yes, that's my story."

"I merely asked you the question."

"I answered it."

"So you did." The DA's eyes came to me. "And of course, Goodwin, your story is the same. If it needed arranging, there was ample time for that during the hubbub that followed Miss Korby's scream. But with you there's more to it. You say that after you and

127

Wolfe re-entered the tent, and he continued through the front entrance to the platform, it occurred to you that there was a possibility that he had taken the paper from his desk and put it in his pocket, and had consulted it during the ride, and had left it in the car, and you went out back again to look, and you were out there when Miss Korby screamed. Is that correct?"

As I had long since decided not to play, when Baxter had got too personal, I merely said, "Check."

Delaney returned to Wolfe. "If you object to my being offensive, Wolfe, I'll put it this way: I find some of this hard to believe. Anyone as glib as you are needing notes for a little speech like that? And you thinking you had left the paper in the car, and Goodwin remembering it had been left at home on your desk and then thinking it might be in the car after all? Also there are certain facts. You and Goodwin were the last people inside the tent before Miss Korby entered and found the body. You admit it. The others all state that they don't know whether the tape was tied or not when they visited the tent; you and Goodwin can't very well say that, since you went out that way, so you say you found it untied."

He cocked his head. "You admit you had had words with Philip Holt during the past year. You admit he had become obnoxious to you—your word, obnoxious—by his insistence that your personal chef must join his union. The record of your past performances justifies me in saying that a man who renders himself obnoxious to you had better watch his step. I'll say this, if it weren't for the probability that some unknown person entered from the rear, and I concede that it's quite possible, you and Goodwin would be held in custody until a judge could be found to issue a warrant for your arrest as material witnesses. As it is, I'll make it easier for you." He looked at his wristwatch. "It's five minutes to eight. I'll send a man with you to a restaurant down the street, and we'll expect you back here at nine-thirty. I want to cover all the details with you, thoroughly." His eyes moved. "The rest of you may go for the present, but you are to be available."

Wolfe stood up. "Mr. Goodwin and I are going home," he announced. "We will not be back this evening."

Delaney's eyes narrowed. "If that's the way you feel about it, you'll stay. You can send out for sandwiches."

"Are we under arrest?"

The DA opened his mouth, closed it, and opened it again. "No."

"Then we're going." Wolfe was assured but not belligerent. "I understand your annoyance, sir, at this interference with your holiday, and I'm aware that you don't like me—or what you know, or think you know, of my record. But I will not surrender my convenience to your humor. You can detain me only if you charge me, and with what? Mr. Goodwin and I have supplied all the information we have. Your intimation that I am capable of murdering a man, or of inciting Mr. Goodwin to murder him, because he has made a nuisance of himself, is puerile. You concede that the murderer could have been anyone in that throng of thousands. You have no basis whatever for any supposition that Mr. Goodwin and I are concealing any knowledge that would help you. Should such a basis appear, you know where to find us. Come, Archie."

He turned and headed for the door, and I followed. I can't report the reaction because Delaney at his desk was behind me, and it would have been bad tactics to look back over my shoulder. All I knew was that Baxter took two steps and stopped, and none of the other cops moved. We made the hall, and the entrance, and down the path to the sidewalk, without a shot being fired; and half a block to where the car was parked. Wolfe told me to find a phone booth and call Fritz to tell him when we would arrive for dinner, and I steered for the center of town.

As I had holiday traffic to cope with, it was half past nine by the time we got home and washed and seated at the dinner table. A moving car is no place to give Wolfe bad news, or good news either for that matter, and there was no point in spoiling his dinner, so I waited until after we had finished with the poached and truffled broilers and broccoli and stuffed potatoes with herbs, and salad and cheese, and Fritz had brought coffee to us in the office, to open the bag. Wolfe was reaching for the remote-control television gadget, to turn it on so as to have the pleasure of turning it off again, when I said, "Hold a minute. I have a report to make. I don't blame you for feeling self-satisfied, you got us away very neatly, but there's a catch. It wasn't somebody that came in the back way. It was one of them."

"Indeed." He was placid, after-dinner placid, in the comfortable big made-to-order chair back of his desk. "What is this, flummery?"

"No, sir. Nor am I trying to show that I'm smarter than you are for once. It's just that I know more. When you left the tent to go to the car your mind was on a quick getaway, so you may not have noticed that a woman was sitting there in a car to the left, but I did. When we returned to the tent and you went on out front, I had an idea and went out back again and had a talk with her. I'll give it to you verbatim, since it's important."

I did so. That was simple, compared with the three-way and four-way conversations I have been called on to report word for word. When I finished he was scowling at me, as black as the coffee in his cup.

"Confound it," he growled.

"Yes, sir. I was going to tell you, there when we were settling the details of why we went out to the car, the paper with your notes, but as you know we were interrupted, and after that there was no opportunity that I liked, and anyway I had seen that Mrs. Banau and the car were gone, and that baboon named Baxter had hurt my feelings, and I had decided not to play. Of course the main thing was you, your wanting to go home. If they had known it was one of us six, or seven counting Flora, we would all have been held as material witnesses, and you couldn't have got bail on the Fourth of July, and God help you, I can manage in a cell, but you're too big. Also if I got you home you might feel like discussing a raise in pay. Do you?"

"Shut up." He closed his eyes, and after a moment

130

opened them again. "We're in a pickle. They may find that woman any moment, or she may disclose herself. What about her? You have given me her words, but what about her?"

"She's good. They'll believe her. I did. You would. From where she sat the steps and tent entrance were in her minimum field of vision, no obstructions, less than ten yards away."

"If she kept her eyes open."

"She thinks she did, and that will do for the cops when they find her. Anyhow, I think she did too. When she said nobody had gone into the tent but you and me she meant it."

"There's the possibility that she herself, or someone she knew and would protect— No, that's absurd, since she stayed there in the car for some time after the body was found. We're in a fix."

"Yes, sir." Meeting his eyes, I saw no sign of the gratitude I might reasonably have expected, so I went on. "I would like to suggest, in considering the situation don't bother about me. I can't be charged with withholding evidence because I didn't report my talk with her. I can just say I didn't believe her and saw no point in making it tougher for us by dragging it in. The fact that someone might have come in the back way didn't eliminate us. Of course I'll have to account for my questioning her, but that's easy. I can say I discovered that he was dead after you went back out to the platform to make your speech, and, having noticed her there in the car, I went out to question her before reporting the discovery, and was interrupted by the scream in the tent. So don't mind me. Anything you say. I can phone Delaney in the morning, or you can, and spill it, or we can just sit tight and wait for the fireworks."

"Pfui," he said.

"Amen," I said.

He took in air, audibly, and let it out. "That woman may be communicating with them at this moment, or they may be finding her. I don't complain of your performance; indeed, I commend it. If you had reported that conversation we would both be spending tonight

131

in jail." He made a face. "Bah. As it is, at least we can try something. What time is it?"

I looked at my wristwatch. He would have had to turn his head almost to a right angle to glance at the wall clock, which was too much to expect. "Eight after eleven."

"Could you get them here tonight?"

"I doubt it. All five of them?"

"Yes."

"Possibly by sunup. Bring them to your bedroom?"

He rubbed his nose with a fingertip. "Very well. But you can call them now, as many as you can get. Make it eleven in the morning. Tell them I have a disclosure to make and must consult with them."

"That should interest them," I granted, and reached for the phone.

IV

By the time Wolfe came down from the plant rooms to greet the guests, at two minutes past eleven the next morning, there hadn't been a peep out of the Long Island law. Which didn't mean there couldn't be one at three minutes past eleven. According to the morning paper, District Attorney Delaney and Chief of Detectives Baxter had both conceded that anyone could have entered the tent from the back and therefore it was wide open. If Anna Banau read newspapers, and she probably did, she might at any moment be going to the phone to make a call.

I had made several, both the night before and that morning, getting the guests lined up; and one special one. There was an address and phone number for an Alexander Banau in the Manhattan book, but I decided not to dial it. I also decided not to ring Zoller's restaurant on Fifty-second Street. I hadn't eaten at Zoller's more than a couple of times, but I knew a man who had been patronizing it for years, and I called him. Yes, he said, there was a captain at Zoller's named Alex, and yes, his last name was Banau. He liked Alex and hoped that my asking about him didn't mean that he was headed for some kind of trouble. I said no trouble was contemplated, I just might want to check a little detail, and thanked him. Then I sat and looked at the slip on which I had scribbled the Banau home phone number, with my finger itching to dial it, but to say what? No.

I mention that around ten-thirty I got the Marley .38 from the drawer, saw that it was loaded, and put it in my side pocket, not to prepare you for bloodshed, but just to show that I was sold on Mrs. Banau. With a murderer for a guest, and an extremely nervy one, there was no telling

H. L. Griffin, the importer, and Paul Rago, the sauce chef, came alone and separately, but Korby and Flora had Dick Vetter with them. I had intended to let Flora have the red leather chair, but when I showed them to the office. Rago, the six-footer with the mustache and the accent, had copped it, and she took one of the yellow chairs in a row facing Wolfe's desk, with her father on her right and Vetter on her left. Griffin, the runt who had made the best speech, was at the end of the row nearest my desk. When Wolfe came down from the plant rooms, entered, greeted them, and headed for his desk, Vetter spoke up before he was seated.

"I hope this won't last long, Mr. Wolfe. I asked Mr. Goodwin if it couldn't be earlier, and he said it couldn't. Miss Korby and I must have an early lunch because I have a script conference at one-thirty."

I raised a brow. I had been honored. I had driven a car with my arm across the shoulders of a girl whom Dick Vetter himself thought worthy of a lunch.

Wolfe, adjusted in his chair, said mildly, "I won't prolong it beyond necessity, sir. Are you and Miss Korby friends?"

"What's that got to do with it?"

"Possibly nothing. But now, nothing about any of you is beyond the bounds of my curiosity. It is a distressing thing to have to say, in view of the occasion of our meeting yesterday, the anniversary of the birth of this land of freedom, but I must. One of you is a miscreant. One of you people killed Philip Holt."

The idea is to watch them and see who faints or jumps up and runs. But nobody did. They all stared.

"One of us?" Griffin demanded.

Wolfe nodded. "I thought it best to begin with that bald statement, instead of leading up to it. I thought—"

Korby cut in. "This is funny. This is a joke. After what you said yesterday to that district attorney. It's a *bad* joke."

"It's no joke, Mr. Korby. I wish it were. I thought yesterday I was on solid ground, but I wasn't. I now

134

know that there is a witness, a credible and confident witness, to testify that no one entered the tent from the rear between the time that the speeches began and the discovery of the body. I also know that neither Mr. Goodwin nor I killed him, so it was one of you. So I think we should discuss it."

"You say a witness?" Rago made it "weetnuss."

"Who is he?" Korby wanted to know. "Where is he?"

"It's a woman, and she is available. Mr. Goodwin, who has spoken with her, is completely satisfied of her competence and bona fides, and he is hard to satisfy. It is highly unlikely that she can be impeached. That's all I—"

"I don't get it," Vetter blurted. "If they've got a witness like that why haven't they come for us?"

"Because they haven't got her. They know nothing about her. But they may find her at any moment, or she may go to them. If so you will soon be discussing the matter not with me but with officers of the law—and so will I. Unless you do discuss it with me, and unless the discussion is productive, I shall of course be constrained to tell Mr. Delaney about her. I wouldn't like that and neither would you. After hearing her story his manner with you, and with me, would be quite different from yesterday. I want to ask you some questions."

"Who is she?" Korby demanded. "Where is she?"

Wolfe shook his head. "I'm not going to identify her or place her for you. I note your expressions—especially yours, Mr. Korby, and yours, Mr. Griffin. You are skeptical. But what conceivable reason could there be for my getting you here to point this weapon at you except the coercion of events? Why would I invent or contrive such a dilemma? I, like you, would vastly prefer to have it as it was, that the murderer came from without, but that's no good now. I concede that you may suspect me too, and Mr. Goodwin, and you may question us as I may question you. But one of us killed Philip Holt, and getting answers to questions is clearly in the interest of all the rest of us."

They exchanged glances But they were not the

kind of glances they would have exchanged five minutes earlier. They were glances of doubt, suspicion, and surmise, and they weren't friendly.

"I don't see," Griffin objected, "what good questions will do. We were all there together and we all know what happened. We all know what everybody said."

Wolfe nodded. "But we were all supporting the theory that excluded us. Now we're not. We can't. One of us has something in his background which, if known, would account for his determination to kill that man. I suggest beginning with autobiographical sketches from each of us, and here is mine. I was born in Montenegro and spent my early boyhood there. At the age of sixteen I decided to move around, and in fourteen years I became acquainted with most of Europe, a little of Africa, and much of Asia, in a variety of roles and activities. Coming to this country in nineteen-thirty, not penniless, I bought this house and entered into practice as a private detective. I am a naturalized American citizen. I first heard of Philip Holt about two years ago when Fritz Brenner, who works for me, came to me with a complaint about him. My only reason for wishing him harm, but not the extremity of death, was removed, as you know, when he agreed to stop annoying Mr. Brenner about joining your union if I would make a speech at your blasted picnic. Mr. Goodwin?"

I turned my face to the audience. "Born in Ohio. Public high school, pretty good at geometry and football, graduated with honor but no honors. Went to college two weeks, decided it was childish, came to New York and got a job guarding a pier, shot and killed two men and was fired, was recommended to Nero Wolfe for a chore he wanted done, did it, was offered a full-time job by Mr. Wolfe, took it, still have it. Personally, was more entertained than bothered by Holt's trying to get union dues out of Fritz Brenner. Otherwise no connection with him or about him."

"You may," Wolfe told them, "question us later if you wish. Miss Korby?"

"Well—" Flora said. She glanced at her father, and,

when he nodded, she aimed at Wolfe and went on, "My autobiography doesn't amount to much. I was born in New York and have always lived here. I'm twenty years old. I didn't kill Phil Holt and had no reason to kill him." She turned her palms up. "What else?"

"If I may suggest," H. L. Griffin offered, "if there's a witness as Wolfe says, if there *is* such a witness, they'll dig everything up. For instance, about you and Phil."

She gave him an eye. "What about us, Mr. Griffin?"

"I don't know. I've only heard talk, that's all, and they'll dig up the talk."

"To hell with the talk," Dick Vetter blurted, the whipped cream sounding sour.

Flora looked at Wolfe. "I can't help talk," she said. "It certainly is no secret that Phil Holt was—well, he liked women. And it's no secret that I'm a woman, and I guess it's not a secret that I didn't like Phil. For me he was what you called him, a nuisance. When he wanted something."

Wolfe grunted. "And he wanted you?"

"He thought he did. That's all there was to it. He was a pest, that's all there is to say about it."

"You said you had no reason to kill him."

"Good heavens, I didn't! A girl doesn't kill a man just because he won't believe her when she says no!"

"No to what? A marriage proposal?"

Her father cut in. "Look here," he told Wolfe, "you're barking up the wrong tree. Everybody knows how Phil Holt was about women. He never asked one to marry him and probably he never would. My daughter is old enough and smart enough to take care of herself, and she does, but not by sticking a knife in a man's back." He turned to Griffin. "Much obliged, Harry."

The importer wasn't fazed. "It was bound to come out, Jim, and I thought it ought to be mentioned now."

Wolfe was regarding Korby. "Naturally it raises the question how far a father might go to relieve his daughter of a pest."

Korby snorted. "If you're asking it, the answer is no. My daughter can take care of herself. If you want a reason why I might have killed Phil Holt you'll have to do better than that."

"Then I'll try, Mr. Korby. You are the president of your union, and Mr. Holt was an important figure in it, and at the moment the affairs of unions, especially their financial affairs, are front-page news. Have you any reason to fear an investigation, or had Mr. Holt?"

"No. They can investigate as much as they damn please."

"Have you been summoned?"

"No."

"Had Mr. Holt been summoned?"

"No."

"Have any officials of your union been summoned?"

"No." Korby's pudgy face and bald top were pinking up a little. "You're barking up the wrong tree again."

"But at least another tree. You realize, sir, that if Mr. Delaney starts after us in earnest, the affairs of the United Restaurant Workers of America will be one of his major concerns. For the murder of Philip Holt we all had opportunity, and the means were there at hand; what he will seek is the motive. If there was a vulnerable spot in the operation of your union, financial or otherwise, I suggest that it would be wise for you to disclose it now for discussion."

"There wasn't anything." Korby was pinker. "There's nothing wrong with my union except rumors. That's all it is, rumors, and where's a union that hasn't got rumors with all the stink they've raised? We're not vulnerable to anything or anybody."

"What kind of rumors?"

"Any kind you want to name. I'm a crook. All the officers are crooks. We've raided the benefit fund. We've sold out to the big operators. We steal lead pencils and paper clips."

"Can you be more specific? What was the most embarrassing rumor?"

Korby was suddenly not listening. He took a folded

138

handkerchief from his pocket, opened it up, wiped his face and his baldness, refolded the handkerchief at the creases, and returned it to his pocket. Then his eyes went back to Wolfe.

"If you want something specific," he said, "it's not a rumor. It's a strictly internal union matter, but it's sure to leak now and it might as well leak here first. There have been some charges made, and they're being looked into, about kickbacks from dealers to union officers and members. Phil Holt had something to do with some of the charges, though that wasn't in his department. He got hot about it."

"Were you the target of any of the charges?"

"I was not. I have the complete trust of my associates and my staff."

"You said 'dealers.' Does that include importers?"

"Sure, importers are dealers."

"Was Mr. Griffin's name mentioned in any of the charges?"

"I'm not giving any names, not without authority from my board. Those things are confidential."

"Much obliged, Jim," H. L. Griffin said, sounding the opposite of obliged. "Even exchange?"

"Excuse me." It was Dick Vetter, on his feet. "It's nearly twelve o'clock and Miss Korby and I have to go. We've got to get some lunch and I can't be late for that conference. Anyway, I think it's a lot of hooey. Come on, Flora."

She hesitated a moment, then left her chair, and he moved. But when Wolfe snapped out his name he turned. "Well?"

Wolfe swiveled his chair. "My apologies. I should have remembered that you are pressed for time. If you can give us, say, five minutes?"

The TV star smiled indulgently. "For my autobiography? You can look it up. It's in print—*TV Guide* a couple of months ago, or *Clock* magazine, I don't remember the date. I say this is hooey. If one of us is a murderer, okay, I wish you luck, but this isn't getting you anywhere. Couldn't I just tell you anything I felt like?"

"You could indeed, Mr. Vetter. But if inquiry reveals that you have lied or have omitted something plainly relevant that will be of interest. The magazine articles you mentioned—do they tell of your interest in Miss Korby?"

"Nuts." Many of his twenty million admirers wouldn't have liked either his tone or his diction.

Wolfe shook his head. "If you insist, Mr. Vetter, you may of course be disdainful about it with me, but not with the police once they get interested in you. I asked you before if you and Miss Korby are friends, and you asked what that had to do with it, and I said possibly nothing. I now say possibly something, since Philip Holt was hounding her—how savagely I don't know yet. Are you and Miss Korby friends?"

"Certainly we're friends. I'm taking her to lunch."

"Are you devoted to her?"

His smile wasn't quite so indulgent, but it was still a smile. "Now that's a delicate question," he said. "I'll tell you how it is. I'm a public figure and I have to watch my tongue. If I said yes, I'm devoted to Miss Korby, it would be in all the columns tomorrow and I'd get ten thousand telegrams and a million letters. If I said no, I'm not devoted to Miss Korby, that wouldn't be polite with her here at my elbow. So I'll just skip it. Come on, Flora."

"One more question. I understand that your father works in a New York restaurant. Do you know whether he is involved in any of the charges Mr. Korby spoke of?"

"Oh, for God's sake. Talk about hooey." He turned and headed for the door, taking Flora with him. I got up and went to the hall and on to the front door, opened it for them, closed it after them, put the chain-bolt on, and returned to the office. Wolfe was speaking.

". . . and I assure you, Mr. Rago, my interest runs with yours—with all of you except one. You don't want the police crawling over you and neither do I."

The sauce chef had straightened up in the red leather chair, and the points of his mustache seemed to have straightened up too. "Treeks," he said.

"No, sir," Wolfe said. "I have no objection to

tricks, if they work, but this is merely a forthright discussion of a lamentable situation. No trick. Do you object to telling us what dealings you had with Philip Holt?"

"I am deesappointed," Rago declared. "Of course I knew you made a living with detective work, everybody knows that, but to me your glory is your great contributions to cuisine—your *sauce printemps*, your oyster pie, your *artichauts drigants*, and others. I know what Pierre Mondor said of you. So it is a deesappointment when I am in your company that the only talk is of the ugliness of murder."

"I don't like it any better than you do, Mr. Rago. I am pleased to know that Pierre Mondor spoke well of me. Now about Philip Holt?"

"If you insist, certainly. But what can I say? Nothing."

"Didn't you know him?"

Rago spread his hands and raised his shoulders and brows. "I had met him. As one meets people. Did I know him? Whom does one know? Do I know you?"

"But you never saw me until two weeks ago. Surely you must have seen something of Mr. Holt. He was an important official of your union, in which you were active."

"I have not been active in the union."

"You were a speaker at its picnic yesterday."

Rago nodded and smiled. "Yes, that is so. But that was because of my activity in the kitchen, not in the union. It may be said, even by me, that in sauces I am supreme. It was for that distinction that it was thought desirable to have me." His head turned. "So, Mr. Korby?"

The president of URWA nodded yes. "That's right," he told Wolfe. "We thought the finest cooking should be represented, and we picked Rago for it. So far as I know, he has never come to a union meeting. We wish he would, and more like him."

"I am a man of the kitchen," Rago declared. "I am an artist. The business I leave to others."

Wolfe was on Korby. "Did Mr. Rago's name appear in any of the charges you spoke of?"

"No. I said I wouldn't give names, but I can say no. No, it didn't."

"You didn't say no when I asked about Mr. Griffin." Wolfe turned to the importer. "Do you wish to comment on that, sir?"

I still hadn't decided exactly what was wrong with Griffin's left eye. There was no sign of an injury, and it seemed to function okay, but it appeared to be a little off center. From an angle, the slant I had from my desk, it looked normal.

He lifted his long narrow chin. "What do you expect?" he demanded.

"My expectations are of no consequence. I merely invite comment."

"On that, I have none. I know nothing about any charges. What I want, I want to see that witness."

Wolfe shook his head. "As I said, I will not produce the witness—for the present. Are you still skeptical?"

"I'm always skeptical." Griffin's voice would have suited a man twice his size. "I want to see that witness and hear what she has to say. I admit I can see no reason why you would invent her—if there is one it's too deep for me, since it puts you in the same boat with us —but I'm not going to believe her until I see her. Maybe I will then, and maybe I won't."

"I think you will. Meanwhile, what about your relations with Philip Holt? How long and how well did you know him?"

"Oh, to hell with this jabber!" Griffin bounced up, not having far to bounce. "If there was anything in my relations with him that made me kill him, would I be telling you?" He flattened his palms on Wolfe's desk. "Are you going to produce that witness? No?" He wheeled. "I've had enough of this! You, Jim? Rago?"

That ended the party. Wolfe could have held Korby and Rago for more jabber, but apparently he didn't think it worth the effort. They asked some questions, what was Wolfe going to do now, and what was the witness going to do, and why couldn't they see her, and why did Wolfe believe her, and was he going to see her and question her, and of course nobody got anything out of that. The atmosphere wasn't very cordial when they left. After letting them out I returned to the office and stood in front of Wolfe's desk. He was leaning back with his arms folded.

"Lunch in twenty minutes," I said cheerfully.

"Not in peace," he growled.

"No, sir. Any instructions?"

"Pfui. It would take an army, and I haven't got one. To go into all of them, to trace all their connections and dealings with the man one of them murdered . . ." He unfolded his arms and put his fists on the desk. "I can't even limit it by assuming that it was an act of urgency, resulting from something that had been said or done that day or in the immediate past. The need or desire to kill him might have dated from a week ago, or a month, or even a year, and it was satisfied yesterday in that tent only because circumstances offered the opportunity. No matter which one it was—Rago, who visited the tent first, or Korby or Griffin or Vetter, who visited it after him in that order—no matter which, the opportunity was tempting. The man was there, recumbent and disabled, and the weapon was there. He had a plausible excuse for entering the tent. To spread the cloud of suspicion to the multitude, all he had to do was untie the tape that held the flap. Even if the body were discovered soon after he left the tent, even seconds after, there would be no question he couldn't answer."

He grunted. "No. Confound it, no. The motive may be buried not only in a complexity of associations but also in history. It might take months. I will have to contrive something."

"Yeah. Any time."

"There may be none. That's the devil of it. Get Saul and Fred and Orrie and have them on call. I have no idea for what, but no matter, get them. And let me alone."

I went to my desk and pulled the phone over.

V

There have been only five occasions in my memory when Wolfe has cut short his afternoon session with the orchids in the plant rooms, from four o'clock to six, and that was the fifth.

If there had been any developments inside his skull I hadn't been informed. There had been none outside, unless you count my calling Saul and Fred and Orrie, our three best bets when we needed outside help, and telling them to stand by. Back at his desk after lunch, Wolfe fiddled around with papers on his desk, counted the week's collection of bottle caps in his drawer, rang for Fritz to bring beer and then didn't drink it, and picked up his current book, *The Fall* by Albert Camus, three or four times, and put it down again. In between he brushed specks of dust from his desk with his little finger. When I turned on the radio for the four-o'clock newscast he waited until it was finished to leave for his elevator trip up to the roof.

Later, nearly an hour later, I caught myself brushing a speck of dust off my desk with my little finger, said something I needn't repeat here, and went to the kitchen for a glass of milk.

When the doorbell rang at a quarter past five I jumped up and shot for the hall, realized that was unmanly, and controlled my legs to a normal gait. Through the one-way glass panel of the front door I saw, out on the stoop, a tall lanky guy, narrow from top to bottom, in a brown suit that needed pressing and a brown straw hat. I took a breath, which I needed apparently, and went and opened the door the two inches allowed by the chain-bolt. His appearance was all against it, but there was no telling what kind of a specimen District Attorney Delaney or Chief of Detectives Baxter might have on his staff.

I spoke through the crack. "Yes, sir?"

"I would like to see Mr. Nero Wolfe. My name is Banau, Alexander Banau."

"Yes, sir." I took the bolt off and swung the door open, and he crossed the sill. "Your hat, sir?" He gave it to me and I put it on the shelf. "This way, sir." I waited until I had him in the office and in the red leather chair to say, "Mr. Wolfe is engaged at the moment. I'll tell him you're here."

I went to the hall and on to the kitchen, shutting doors on the way, buzzed the plant rooms on the house phone, and in three seconds, instead of the usual fifteen or twenty, had a growl in my ear. "Yes?"

"Company. Captain Alexander Banau."

Silence, then: "Let him in."

"He's already in. Have you any suggestions how I keep him occupied until six o'clock?"

"No." A longer silence. "I'll be down."

As I said, that was the fifth time in all the years I have been with him. I went back to the office and asked the guest if he would like something to drink, and he said no, and in two minutes there was the sound of Wolfe's elevator descending and stopping, the door opening and shutting, and his tread. He entered, circled around the red leather chair, and offered a hand.

"Mr. Banau? I'm Nero Wolfe. How do you do, sir?"

He was certainly spreading it on. He doesn't like to shake hands, and rarely does. When he was adjusted in his chair he gave Banau a look so sociable it was damn close to fawning, for him.

"Well, sir?"

"I fear," Banau said, "that I may have to make myself disagreeable. I don't like to be disagreeable. Is that gentleman"—he nodded at me—"Mr. Archie Goodwin?"

"He is, yes, sir."

"Then it will be doubly disagreeable, but it can't be

helped. It concerns the tragic event at Culp's Meadows yesterday. According to the newspaper accounts, the police are proceeding on the probability that the murderer entered the tent from the rear, and left that way after he had performed the deed. Just an hour ago I telephoned to Long Island to ask if they still regard that as probable, and was told that they do."

He stopped to clear his throat. I would have liked to get my fingers around it to help. He resumed.

"It is also reported that you and Mr. Goodwin were among those interviewed, and that compels me to conclude, reluctantly, that Mr. Goodwin has failed to tell you of a conversation he had with my wife as she sat in our car outside the tent. I should explain that I was in the crowd in front, and when your speech was interrupted by the scream, and confusion resulted, I made my way around to the car, with some difficulty, and got in and drove away. I do not like tumult. My wife did not tell me of her conversation with Mr. Goodwin until after we got home. She regards it as unwise to talk while I am driving. What she told me was that Mr. Goodwin approached the car and spoke to her through the open window. He asked her if anyone—"

"If you please." Wolfe wiggled a finger. "Your assumption that he hasn't reported the conversation to me is incorrect. He has."

"What! He has?"

"Yes, sir. If you will—"

"Then you know that my wife is certain that no one entered the tent from the rear while the speeches were being made? No one but you and Mr. Goodwin? Absolutely certain? You know she told him that?"

"I know what she told him, yes. But if you will—"

"And you haven't told the police?"

"No, not yet. I would like—"

"Then she has no choice." Banau was on his feet. "It is even more disagreeable than I feared. She must communicate with them at once. This is terrible, a man of your standing, and the others too. It is terrible, but it must be done. In a country of law the law must be served."

He turned and headed for the door.

I left my chair. Stopping him and wrapping him up would have been no problem, but I was myself stopped by the expression on Wolfe's face. He looked relieved; he even looked pleased. I stared at him, and was still staring when the sound came of the front door closing. I stepped to the hall, saw that he was gone and hadn't forgotten his hat, and returned and stood at Wolfe's desk.

"Goody," I said. "Cream? Give me some."

He took in air, all the way, and let it out. "This is more like it," he declared. "I've had all the humiliation I can stand. Jumping out of my skin every time the phone rang. Did you notice how quickly I answered your ring upstairs? Afraid, by heaven, afraid to go into the tropical room to look over the Renanthera imschootiana! Now we know where we are."

"Yeah. Also where we soon will be. If it had been me I would have kept him at least long enough to tell him—"

"Shut up."

I did so. There are certain times when it is understood that I am not to badger, and the most important is when he leans back in his chair and shuts his eyes and his lips start to work. He pushes them out, pulls them in, out and in, out and in. . . . That means his brain has crashed the sound barrier. I have seen him, dealing with a tough one, go on with that lip action for up to an hour. I sat down at my desk, thinking I might as well be near the phone.

That time he didn't take an hour, not having one. More like eight minutes. He opened his eyes, straightened up, and spoke.

"Archie. Did he tell you where his wife was?"

"No. He told me nothing. He was saving it for you. She could have been in the drugstore at the corner, sitting in the phone booth."

He grunted. "Then we must clear out of here. I am going to find out which of them killed that man before we are all hauled in. The motive and the evidence will have to come later; the thing now is to identify him as a bone to toss to Mr. Delaney. Where is Saul?"

"At home, waiting to hear. Fred and Orrie—"

"We need only Saul. Call him. Tell him we are coming there at once. Where would Mr. Vetter have his conference?"

"I suppose at the MXO studio."

"Get him. And if Miss Korby is there, her also. And the others. You must get them all before they hear from Mr. Delaney. They are all to be at Saul's place without delay. At the earliest possible moment. Tell them they are to meet and question the witness, and it is desperately urgent. If they balk I'll speak to them and—"

I had the phone, dialing.

VI

After they were all there and Wolfe started in, it took him less than fifteen minutes to learn which one was it. I might have managed it in fifteen days, with luck. If you like games you might lean back now, close your eyes and start pushing your lips out and in, and see how long it takes you to decide how you would do it. Fair enough, since you know everything that Wolfe and I knew. But get it straight; don't try to name him or come up with evidence that would nail him; the idea is, how do you use what you now know to put the finger on him? That was what Wolfe did, and I wouldn't expect more of you than of him.

Saul Panzer, below average in size but miles above it in savvy, lived alone on the top floor—living room, bedroom, kitchenette, and bath—of a remodeled house on Thirty-eighth Street between Lexington and Third. The living room was big, lighted with two floor lamps and two table lamps, even at seven o'clock of a July evening, because the blinds were drawn. One wall had windows, another was solid with books, and the other two had pictures and shelves that were cluttered with everything from chunks of minerals to walrus tusks. In the far corner was a grand piano.

Wolfe sent his eyes around and said, "This shouldn't take long."

He was in the biggest chair Saul had, by a floor lamp, almost big enough for him. I was on a stool to his left and front, and Saul was off to his right, on the piano bench. The chairs of the five customers were in an arc facing him. Of course it would have been sensible and desirable to arrange the seating so that the murderer was next to either Saul or me, but that wasn't practical since we had no idea which one it was, and neither did Wolfe.

"Where's the witness?" Griffin demanded. "Goodwin said she'd be here."

Wolfe nodded. "I know. Mr. Goodwin is sometimes careless with his pronouns. The witness is present." He aimed a thumb at the piano bench. "There. Mr. Saul Panzer, who is not only credible and confident but—"

"You said it was a woman!"

"There is another witness who is a woman; doubtless there will be others when one of you goes on trial. The urgency Mr. Goodwin spoke of relates to what Mr. Panzer will tell you. Before he does so, some explanation is required."

"Let him talk first," Dick Vetter said, "and then explain. We've heard from you already."

"I'll make it brief." Wolfe was unruffled. "It concerns the tape fastening on the flap of the rear entrance of the tent. As you know, Mr. Goodwin tied it before we left to go to the platform, and when he and I entered the tent later and left by the rear entrance it had been untied. By whom? Not by someone entering from the outside, since there is a witness to testify that no one had—"

James Korby cut in. "That's the witness we want to see. Goodwin said she'd be here."

"You'll see her, Mr. Korby, in good time. Please bear with me. Therefore the tape had been untied by someone who had entered from the front—by one of you four men. Why? The presumption is overwhelming that it was untied by the murderer, to create and support the probability that Philip Holt had been stabbed by someone who entered from the rear. It is more than a presumption; it approaches certainty. So it seemed to me that it was highly desirable, if possible, to learn who had untied the tape; and I enlisted the services of Mr. Panzer." His head turned. "Saul, if you please?"

Saul had his hand on a black leather case beside

him on the bench. "Do you want it all, Mr. Wolfe? How I got it?"

"Not at the moment, I think. Later, if they want to know. What you have is more important than how you got it."

"Yes, sir." He opened the lid of the case and took something from it. "I'd rather not explain how I got it because it might make trouble for somebody."

I horned in. "What do you mean 'might'? You know damn well it would make trouble for somebody."

"Okay, Archie, okay." His eyes went to the audience. "What I've got is these photographs of fingerprints that were lifted from the tape on the flap of the rear entrance of the tent. There are some blurry ones, but there are four good ones. Two of the good ones are Mr. Goodwin's, and that leaves two unidentified." He turned to the case and took things out. He cocked his head to the audience. "The idea is, I take your prints and—"

"Not so fast, Saul." Wolfe's eyes went right, and left again. "You see how it is, and you understand why Mr. Goodwin said it was urgent. Surely those of you who did *not* untie the tape will not object to having your prints compared with the photographs. If anyone does object he cannot complain if an inference is made. Of course there is the possibility that none of your prints will match the two unidentified ones in the photographs, and in that case the results will be negative and not conclusive. Mr. Panzer has the equipment to take your prints, and he is an expert. Will you let him?"

Glances were exchanged.

"What the hell," Vetter said. "Mine are on file anyway. Sure."

"Mine also," Griffin said. "I have no objection."

Paul Rago abruptly exploded. "Treeks again!"

All eyes went to him. Wolfe spoke. "No, Mr. Rago, no tricks. Mr. Panzer would prefer not to explain how he got the photographs, but he will if you insist. I assure you—"

151

"I don't mean treeks how he gets them." The sauce chef uncrossed his legs. "I mean what you said, it was the murderer who untied the tape. That is not necessary. I can say that was a lie! When I entered the tent and looked at him it seemed to me he did not breathe good, there was not enough air, and I went and untied the tape so the air could come through. So if you take my print and find it is like the photograph, what will that prove? Nothing at all. Nuh-theeng! So I say it is treeks again, and in this great land of freedom—"

I wasn't trying to panic him. I wasn't even going to touch him. And I had the Marley .38 in my pocket, and Saul had one too, so if he had tried to start something he would have got stopped quick. But using a gun, especially in a crowd, is always bad management unless you have to, and he was twelve feet away from me, and I got up and moved merely because I wanted to be closer. Saul had the same notion at the same instant, and the sight of us two heading for him, with all that he knew that we didn't know yet, was too much for him. He was out of his chair and plunging toward the door as I took my second step.

Then, of course, we had to touch him. I reached him first, not because I'm faster than Saul but because he was farther off. And the damn fool put up a fight, although I had him wrapped. He kicked Saul where it hurt, and knocked a lamp over, and bumped my nose with his skull. When he sank his teeth in my arm I thought, That will do for you, mister, and jerked the Marley from my pocket and slapped him above the ear, and he went down.

Turning, I saw that Dick Vetter had also wrapped his arms around someone, and she was neither kicking nor biting. In moments of stress people usually show what is really on their minds, even important public figures like TV stars. There wasn't a word about it in the columns next day.

152

VII

I have often wondered how Paul Rago felt when, at his trial a couple of months later, no evidence whatever was introduced about fingerprints. He knew then, of course, that it had been a treek and nothing but, that no prints had been lifted from the tape by Saul or anyone else, and that if he had kept his mouth shut and played along he might have been playing yet.

I once asked Wolfe what he would have done if that had happened.

He said, "It didn't happen."

I said, "What if it had?"

He said, "Pfui. The contigency was too remote to consider. It was as good as certain that the murderer had untied the tape. Confronted with the strong probability that it was about to be disclosed that his print was on the tape, he had to say something. He had to explain how it got there, and it was vastly preferable to do so voluntarily instead of waiting until evidence compelled it."

I hung on. "Okay, it was a good trick, but I still say what if?"

"And I still say it is pointless to consider remote contingencies. What if your mother had abandoned you in a tiger's cage at the age of three months? What would you have done?"

I told him I'd think it over and let him know.

As for motive, you can have three guesses if you want them, but you'll never get warm if you dig them out of what I have reported. In all the jabber in Wolfe's office that day, there wasn't one word that had the slightest bearing on why Philip Holt died, which goes to show why detectives get ulcers. No, I'm wrong; it was mentioned that Philip Holt liked women, and certainly that had a bearing. One of the women he had liked was Paul Rago's wife, an attractive blue-eyed number about half as old as her husband, and he was still liking her, and, unlike Flora Korby, she had liked him and proved it.

Paul Rago hadn't liked that.

Murder
Is No Joke

I

I was a little disappointed in Flora Gallant when she arrived that Tuesday morning for her eleven-o'clock appointment with Nero Wolfe. Her getup was a letdown. One of my functions as Wolfe's factotum is checking on people who phone for an appointment with him, and when I had learned that Flora Gallant was one of the staff of her brother Alec's establishment on East Fifty-fourth Street, and remembered remarks a friend of mine named Lily Rowan had made about Alec Gallant, I had phoned Lily for particulars.

And got them. Gallant was crowding two others for top ranking in the world of high fashion. He thumbed his nose at Paris and sneered at Rome, and was getting away with it. He had refused to finish three dresses for the Duchess of Harwynd because she postponed flying over from London for fittings. He declined to make anything whatever for a certain famous movie actress because he didn't like the way she handled her hips when she walked. He had been known to charge as little as eight hundred dollars for an afternoon frock, but it had been for a favorite customer so he practically gave it away.

And so forth. Therefore when I opened the door to admit his sister Flora that Tuesday morning it was a letdown to see a dumpy middle-aged female in a dark gray suit that was anything but spectacular. It needed pressing, and the shoulders were too tight, and her waist wasn't where it thought it was. As I ushered her down the hall to the office and introduced her to Wolfe, I was thinking that if the shoemaker's son went barefoot I supposed his sister could too, but all the same I felt cheated.

Her conversation was no more impressive than her costume, at least at the beginning. Seated on the edge of the red leather chair beyond the end of Wolfe's desk, the fingers of both hands gripping the rim of the gray leather bag on her lap, she apologized, in a low meek mumble with just a trace of a foreign accent, for asking such an important man as Nero Wolfe to give any of his valuable time to her and her troubles. That didn't sound promising, indicating as it did that she was looking for a bargain. As she went on with it Wolfe started a frown going, and soon he cut her off by saying that it would take less of his time if she would tell him what her troubles were.

She nodded. "I know. I just wanted you to understand that I don't expect anything for myself. I'm not anybody myself, but you know who my brother is? My brother Alec?"

"Yes. Mr. Goodwin has informed me. An illustrious dressmaker."

"He is not merely a dressmaker. He is an artist, a great artist." She wasn't arguing, just stating a fact. "This trouble is about him, and that's why I must be careful with it. That's why I come to you, and also" —she sent me a glance and then back to Wolfe—"also Mr. Archie Goodwin, because I know that although you are private detectives, you are gentlemen. I know you are worthy of confidence."

She stopped, apparently for acknowledgment. Wolfe obliged her. "Umph."

"Then it is understood I am trusting you?"

"Yes. You may."

She looked at me. "Mr. Goodwin?"

"Right. Whatever Mr. Wolfe says. I only work here."

She hesitated, seeming to consider if that was satisfactory, decided it was, and returned to Wolfe. "So I'll tell you. I must explain that in France, where my brother and I were born and brought up, our name was not 'Gallant.' What it was doesn't matter. I came to this country in nineteen-thirty-seven, when I was twenty five years old, and Alec only came in nineteen-forty-five, after the war was over. He had changed his name to Gallant and entered legally under that name. Within seven years he had made a reputation as a designer, and then— Perhaps you remember his fall collection in nineteen-fifty-three?"

Wolfe grunted no.

Her right hand abandoned its grip on the bag to gesture. "But of course you are not married, and you have no mistress, feeling as you do about women. That collection showed what my brother was—an artist, a true creator. He got financial backing, more than he needed, and opened his place on Fifty-fourth Street. I had quit my job four years earlier—my job as a governess—in order to work with him and help him, and had changed my name to have it the same as his. From nineteen-fifty-three on it has been all a triumph, many triumphs. I will not say I had a hand in them, but I have been trying to help in my little way. The glory of great success has been my brother's, but I have been with him, and so have others. But now trouble has come."

Both hands were gripping the bag again. "The trouble," she said, "is a woman. A woman named Bianca Voss."

Wolfe made a face. She saw it and responded to it. "No, not an *affaire d'amour*, I'm sure it's not that. Though my brother has never married, he is by no means insensible to women, he is very healthy about women, but since you are worthy of confidence I may tell you that he has an *amie intime*, a young woman who is of importance in his establishment. It is impossible that Bianca Voss has attracted him that way. She first came there a little more than a year ago. My brother had told us to expect her, so he had met her somewhere. He designed a dress and a suit for her, and they were made there in the shop, but no bill was ever sent her. Then he gave her one of the rooms, the offices, on the third floor, and she started to come every day, and then the trouble began. My brother never told us she had any authority, but she took it and he allowed her to. Sometimes she interferes directly, and sometimes through him. She pokes her nose into everything. She got my brother to discharge a fitter, a very

159

capable woman, who had been with him for years. She has a private telephone line in her office upstairs, but no one else has. About two months ago some of the others persuaded me to try to find out about her, what her standing is, and I asked my brother, but he wouldn't tell me. I begged him to, but he wouldn't."

"It sounds," Wolfe said, "as if she owns the business. Perhaps she bought it."

Flora Gallant shook her head. "No, she hasn't. I'm sure she hasn't. She wasn't one of the financial backers in nineteen-fifty-three, and since then there have been good profits, and anyway my brother has control. But now she's going to ruin it and he's going to let her, we don't know why. She wants him to design a factory line to be promoted by a chain of department stores using his name. She wants him to sponsor a line of Alec Gallant cosmetics on a royalty basis. And other things. We're against all of them, and my brother is too, really, but we think he's going to give in to her, and that will ruin it."

Her fingers tightened on the bag. "Mr. Wolfe, I want you to ruin *her.*"

Wolfe grunted. "By wiggling a finger?"

"No, but you can. I'm sure you can. I'm sure she has some hold on him, but I don't know what. I don't know who she is or where she came from. I don't know what her real name is. She speaks with an accent, but not French; I'm not sure what it is. I don't know when she came to America; she may be here illegally. She may have known my brother in France, during the war. You can find out. If she has a hold on my brother you can find out what it is. If she is blackmailing him, isn't that against the law? Wouldn't that ruin her?"

"It might. It might ruin him too."

"Not unless you betrayed him." She swallowed that and added hastily, "I don't mean that, I only mean I am trusting you, you said I could, and you could make her stop and that's all you would have to do. Couldn't you just do that?"

"Conceivably." Wolfe wasn't enthusiastic. "I fear, madam, that you're biting off more than you can chew. The procedure you suggest would be prolonged, laborious, and extremely expensive. It would probably require elaborate investigation abroad. Aside from my fee, which would not be modest, the outlay would be considerable and the outcome highly uncertain. Are you in a position to undertake it?"

"I am not rich myself, Mr. Wolfe. I have some savings. But my brother—if you get her away, if you release him from her—he is truly *générlux*—excuse me —he is a generous man. He is not stingy."

"But he isn't hiring me, and your assumption that she is galling him may be groundless." Wolfe shook his head. "No. Not a reasonable venture. Unless, of course, your brother himself consults me. If you care to bring him? Or send him?"

"Oh, I couldn't!" She gestured again. "You must see that isn't possible! When I asked him about her, I told you, he wouldn't tell me anything. He was annoyed. He is never abrupt with me, but he was then. I assure you, Mr. Wolfe, she is a villain. You are *sagace* —excuse me—you are an acute man. You would know it if you saw her, spoke with her."

"Perhaps." Wolfe was getting impatient. "Even so, my perception of her villainy wouldn't avail. No, madam."

"But you would know I am right." She opened her bag, fingered in it with both hands, came out with something, left her chair to step to Wolfe's desk, and put the something on his desk pad in front of him. "There," she said, "that is one hundred dollars. For you that is nothing, but it shows how I am in earnest. I can't ask her to come so you can speak with her, she would merely laugh at me, but you can. You can tell her you have been asked in confidence to discuss a matter with her and ask her to come to see you. You will not tell her what it is. She will come, she will be afraid not to, and that alone will show you she has a secret, perhaps many secrets. Then when she comes you will ask her whatever occurs to you. For that you do not need my suggestions. You are an acute man."

Wolfe grunted. "Everybody has secrets."

"Yes," she agreed, "but not secrets that would

make them afraid not to come to see Nero Wolfe. When she comes and you have spoken with her, we shall see. That may be all or it may not. We shall see."

I do not say that the hundred bucks there on his desk in used twenties was no factor in Wolfe's decision. Even though income tax would reduce it to sixteen dollars, that would buy four days' supply of beer. Another factor was plain curiosity: would she come or wouldn't she? Still another was the chance that it might develop into a decent fee. But what really settled it was her saying, "We shall see" instead of "We'll see" or "We will see." He will aways stretch a point, within reason, for people who use words as he thinks they should be used. So he muttered at her, "Where is she?"

"At my brother's place. She always is."

"Give Mr. Goodwin the phone number."

"I'll get it. She may be downstairs." She started a hand for the phone on Wolfe's desk, but I told her to use mine and left my chair, and she came and sat, lifted the receiver, and dialed.

In a moment she spoke. "Doris? Flora. Is Miss Voss around? . . . Oh. I thought she might have come down. . . . No, don't bother, I'll ring her there."

She pushed the button down, told us, "She's up in her office," waited a moment, released the button, and dialed again. When she spoke it was another voice, as she barely moved her lips and brought it out through her nose: "Miss Bianca Voss? Hold the line, please. Mr. Nero Wolfe wishes to speak with you. . . . Mr. Nero Wolfe, the private detective."

She looked at Wolfe and he got at his phone. Having my own share of curiosity, I extended a hand for my receiver, and she let me take it and left my chair. As I sat and got it to my ear Wolfe was speaking.

"This is Nero Wolfe. Is this Miss Bianca Voss?"

"Yes." It was more like "yiss." "What do you want?" The "wh" and the "w" were off.

"If my name is unknown to you, I should explain—"

"I know your name. What do you want?"

"I want to invite you to call on me at my office. I

162

have been asked to discuss certain matters with you, and—"

"Who asked you?"

"I am not at liberty to say. I shall—"

"What matters?" The "wh" was more off.

"If you will let me finish. The matters are personal and confidential, and concern you closely. That's all I can say on the telephone. I am sure you—"

A snort stopped him, a snort that might be spelled "Tzchaahh!" followed by: "I know your name, yes! You are scum, I know, in your stinking sewer! Your slimy little ego in your big gob of fat! And you dare to—*owulggh!*"

That's the best I can do at spelling it. It was part scream, part groan, and part just noise. It was followed immediately by another noise, a mixture of crash and clatter, then others, faint rustlings, and then nothing. I looked at Wolfe and he looked at me. I spoke to my transmitter. "Hello hello hello. *Hello!* Hello?"

I cradled it and so did Wolfe. Flora Gallant was asking, "What is it? She hung up?"

We ignored her. Wolfe said, "Archie? You heard."

"Yes, sir. If you want a guess, something hit her and she dragged the phone along as she went down and it struck the floor. The other noises, not even a guess, except that at the end either she put the receiver back on and cut the connection or someone else did. I don't — Okay, Miss Gallant. Take it easy." She had grabbed my arm with both hands and was jabbering, "What is it? What happened?" I put a hand on her shoulder and made it emphatic. "Take a breath and let go. You heard what I told Mr. Wolfe. Apparently something fell on her and then hung up the phone."

"But it couldn't! It is not possible!"

"That's what it sounded like. What's the number? The one downstairs?"

She just gawked at me. I looked at Wolfe and he gave me a nod, and I jerked my arm loose, sat at my desk, got the Manhattan book, flipped to the Gs and got the number, PL2–0330, and dialed it.

A cultured female voice came. "Alec Gallant Incorporated."

"This is a friend of Miss Voss," I told her. "I was just speaking to her on the phone, in her office, and from the sounds I got I think something may have happened to her. Will you send someone up to see? Right away. I'll hold the wire."

"Who is this speaking, please?"

"Never mind that. Step on it. She may be hurt."

I heard her calling to someone, then apparently she covered the transmitter. I sat and waited. Wolfe sat and scowled at me. Flora Gallant stood for a good five minutes at my elbow, staring down at me, then turned and went to the red leather chair and lowered herself onto its edge. I looked at my wristwatch: 11:40. It had said 11:31 when the connection with Bianca Voss had been cut. More waiting, and then a male voice came.

"Hello?"

"Hello."

"This is Carl Drew. What is your name, please?"

"My name is Watson, John H. Watson. Is Miss Voss all right?"

"May I have your address, Mr. Watson, please?"

"What for? Miss Voss knows my address. Is she all right?"

"I must have your address, Mr. Watson. I must insist. You will understand the necessity when I tell you that Miss Voss is dead. She was assaulted in her office and is dead. Apparently, from what you said, the assault came while she was on the phone with you, and I want your address. I must insist."

I hung up, gently not to be rude, swiveled, and asked Flora Gallant, "Who is Carl Drew?"

"He's the business manager. What happened?"

I went to Wolfe. "My guess was close. Miss Voss is dead. In her office. He said she was assaulted, but he didn't say with what or by whom."

He glowered at me, then turned to let her have it. She was coming up from the chair, slow and stiff. When she was erect she said, "No. No. It isn't possible."

"I'm only quoting Carl Drew," I told her.

"It isn't possible. He said that?"

"Distinctly."

But how—" She let it hang. She said, "But how —" stopped again, turned, and was going. When Wolfe called to her, "Here, Miss Gallant, your money," she paid no attention but kept on, and he poked it at me, and I took it and headed for the hall. I caught up with her halfway to the front door, but when I offered it she just kept going, so I blocked her off, took her bag and opened it and dropped the bills in and closed it, handed it back, and went and pulled the door open. She hadn't said a word. I stood on the sill and watched, thinking she might stumble going down the seven steps of the stoop, but she made it to the sidewalk and turned east, toward Ninth Avenue. When I got back to the office Wolfe was sitting with his eyes closed, breathing down to his big round middle. I went to my desk and put the phone book away.

"She is so stunned with joy," I remarked, "that she'll probably get run over. I should have gone and put her in a taxi."

He grunted.

"One thing," I remarked, "Miss Voss's last words weren't exactly *généreux*. I would call them catty."

He grunted.

"Another thing," I remarked, "in spite of the fact that I was John H. Watson on the phone, we'll certainly be called on by either Sergeant Stebbins or Inspector Cramer or both. When they go into whereabouts Flora will have to cough it up for her own protection. And we actually heard it. Also we'll have the honor of being summoned to the stand. Star witnesses."

He opened his eyes. "I'm quite aware of it," he growled. "Confound it. Bring me the records on Laelia gouldiana."

No orchid ever called a genius a slimy little ego in a big gob of fat. I remarked that too, but to myself.

II

"Sure I appreciate it," Cramer declared. "Why shouldn't I? Very thoughful of you. Saves me time and trouble. So it was eleven-thirty-one when you heard the blow?"

Inspector Cramer, big and brawny with a round red face and all his hair, half of it gray, had nothing to be sarcastic about as he sat in the red leather chair at six-thirty that Tuesday afternoon, and he knew it, but he couldn't help it. It was his reaction, not to the present circumstances, but to his memory of other occasions, other experiences he had undergone in that room. He had to admit that we had saved him time and trouble when I had anticipated his visit by typing out a complete report of the session with Flora Gallant that morning, including the dialogue verbatim, and having it ready for him in duplicate, signed by both Wolfe and me. He had skimmed through it first, and then read it slowly and carefully.

"We heard no blow, identifiably," Wolfe objected. His bulk was comfortably arranged in his oversize chair back of his desk. "Mr. Goodwin wrote that statement, but I read it, and it does not say that we heard a blow."

Cramer found the place on page four and consulted it. "Okay. You heard a groan and a crash and rustles. But there *was* a blow. She was hit in the back of the head with a chunk of marble, a paperweight, and then a scarf was tied around her throat to stop her breathing. You say here at eleven-thirty-one."

"Not when we heard the groan," I corrected. "After that there were the other noises, then the

166

connection went, and I said hello a few times, which was human but dumb. It was when I hung up that I looked at my watch and saw eleven-thirty-one. The groan had been maybe a minute earlier. Say eleven-thirty. If a minute is important."

"It isn't. But you didn't hear the blow?"

"Not to recognize it, no."

He went back to the statement, frowning at it, reading the whole first page and glancing at the others. He looked up, at Wolfe. "I know how good you are at arranging words. This implies that Flora Gallant was a complete stranger to you, that you had never had anything to do with her or her brother or any of the people at that place, but it doesn't say so in so many words. I'd like to know."

"The implication is valid," Wolfe told him. "Except as related in that statement, I have never had any association with Miss Gallant or her brother, or, to my knowledge, with any of their colleagues. Nor has Mr. Goodwin. Archie?"

"Right," I agreed.

"Okay." Cramer folded the statement and put it in his pocket. "Then you had never heard Bianca Voss's voice before and you couldn't recognize it on the phone."

"Of course not."

"And you can't hear it now, since she's dead. So you can't swear it was her talking to you."

"Obviously."

"And that raises a point. If it was her talking to you, she was killed at exactly half past eleven. Now there are four important people in that organization who had it in for Bianca Voss. They have admitted it. Besides Flora Gallant, there is Anita Prince, fitter and designer, been with Gallant eight years; Emmy Thorne, in charge of contacts and promotion, been with him four years; and Carl Drew, business manager, been with him five years. None of them killed Bianca Voss at half past eleven. From eleven-fifteen on, until the call came from a man who said he was John H. Watson, Carl Drew was down on the main floor, constantly in view of four people, two of them customers.

From eleven o'clock on Anita Prince was on the top floor, the workshop, with Alec Gallant and two models and a dozen employees. At eleven-twenty Emmy Thorne called on a man by appointment at his office on Forty-sixth Street, and was with him and two other men until a quarter to twelve. And Flora Gallant was here with you. All airtight."

"Very neat," Wolfe agreed.

"Yeah. Too damn neat. Of course there may be others who wanted Bianca Voss out of the way, but as it stands now those four are out in front. And they're all—"

"Why not five? Alec Gallant himself?"

"All right, five. They're all in the clear, including him, if she was killed at eleven-thirty. So suppose she wasn't. Suppose she was killed earlier, half an hour or so earlier. Suppose when Flora Gallant phoned her from here and put you on to talk with her, it wasn't her at all, it was someone else imitating her voice, and she pulled that stunt, the groan and the other noises, to make you think you had heard the murder at that time."

Wolfe's brows were up. "With the corpse there on the floor."

"Certainly."

"Then you're not much better off. Who did the impersonation? Their alibis still hold for eleven-thirty."

"I realize that. But there were nineteen women around there altogether, and a woman who wouldn't commit a murder might be willing to help cover up after it had been committed. You know that."

Wolfe wasn't impressed. "It's very tricky, Mr. Cramer. If you are supposing Flora Gallant killed her, it was elaborately planned. Miss Gallant phoned here yesterday morning to make an appointment for eleven this morning. Did she kill Miss Voss, station someone there beside the corpse to answer the phone, rush down here, and maneuver me into ringing Miss Voss's number? It seems a little far-fetched."

"I didn't say it was Flora Gallant." Cramer hung on. "It could have been any of them. He or she didn't have to know you were going to ring that number. He might have intended to call it himself, before witnesses, to establish the time of the murder, and when your call came, whoever it was there by the phone got rattled and went ahead with the act. There are a dozen different ways it could have happened. Hell, I know it's tricky. I'm not asking you to work your brain on it. You must know why I brought it up."

Wolfe nodded. "Yes, I think I do. You want me to consider what I heard—and Mr. Goodwin. You want to know if we are satisfied that those sounds were authentic. You want to know if we will concede that they might have been bogus."

"That's it. Exactly."

Wolfe rubbed his nose with a knuckle, closing his eyes. In a moment he opened them. "I'm afraid I can't help you, Mr. Cramer. If they were bogus they were well executed. At the time, hearing them, I had no suspicion that it was flummery. Naturally, as soon as I learned that they served to fix the precise moment of a murder, I knew they were open to question, but I can't challenge them intrinsically. Archie?"

I shook my head. "I pass." To Cramer: "You've read the statement, so you know that right after I heard it my guess was that something hit her and she dragged the phone along as she went down and it struck the floor. I'm not going to go back on my guess now. As for our not hearing the blow, read the statement. It says that it started out as if it was going to be a scream but then it was a groan. She might have seen the blow coming and was going to scream, but it landed and turned it into a groan, and in that case we wouldn't hear the blow. A chunk of marble hitting a skull wouldn't make much noise. As for supposing she was killed half an hour or so earlier, I phoned within three minutes, or John H. Watson did, and in another six or seven minutes Carl Drew was talking to me, so he must have seen the body, or someone did, not more than five minutes after we heard the groan. Was she twitching?"

"No. You don't twitch long with a scarf as tight as that around your throat."

"What about the ME?"

"He got there a little after twelve. With blood he might have timed it pretty close, but there wasn't any. That's out."

"What about the setup? Someone left that room quick after we heard the sounds. If it was the murderer, he or she had to cradle the phone and tie the scarf, but that wouldn't take long. If it was a fill-in, as you want to suppose, all she had to do was cradle the phone. Whichever it was, wasn't there anyone else around?"

"No. If there was, they're saving it. As you know, Bianca Voss wasn't popular around there. Anyway, that place is a mess, with three different elevators, one in the store, one at the back for services and deliveries, and one in an outside hall with a separate entrance so they can go up to the offices without going through the store."

"That makes it nice. Then it's wide open."

"As wide as a barn door." Cramer stood up. To Wolfe: "So that's the best you can do. You thought the sounds were open to question."

"Not intrinsically. Circumstantially, of course."

"Yeah. Much obliged." He was going. After two steps he turned. "I don't like gags about homicide, murder is no joke, but I can mention that Bianca Voss had you wrong. Scum. Stinking sewer. Orchids don't smell." He went.

Apparently he hadn't really swallowed it that she was already dead when we heard the sounds.

III

The next morning, Wednesday, eating breakfast in the kitchen with the *Times* propped up in front of me, which is routine, of course I read the account of the Bianca Voss murder. There were various details that were news to me, but nothing startling or even helpful. It included the phone call from John H. Watson, but didn't add that he had been identified as Archie Goodwin, and there was no mention of Nero Wolfe. I admit that the cops and the DA have a right to save something for themselves, but it never hurts to have your name in the paper, and I had a notion to phone Lon Cohen at the *Gazette* and give him an exclusive. However, I would have to mention it to Wolfe first, so it would have to wait until eleven o'clock.

As a matter of fact, another item in the *Times* came closer to me. Sarah Yare had committed suicide. Her body had been found Tuesday evening in her little walk-up apartment on East Thirteenth Street. I had never written a fan letter to an actress, but I had been tempted to a couple of years back when I had seen Sarah Yare in *Thumb a Ride*. The first time I saw it I had a companion, but the next three times I was alone. The reason for repeating was that I had the impression I was infatuated and I wanted to wear it down, but when the impression still stuck after three tries I quit. Actresses should be seen and heard, but not touched. At that, I might have given the impression another test in a year or two if there had been an opportunity, but there wasn't. She quit *Thumb a Ride* abruptly some months later, and the talk was that she was an alco and done for.

171

So I read that item twice. It didn't say that it had been pronounced suicide officially and finally, since she had left no note, but a nearly empty bourbon bottle had been there on a table, and on the floor by the couch she had died on there had been a glass with enough left in it to identify the cyanide. The picture of her was as she had been when I had got my impression. I asked Fritz if he had ever seen Sarah Yare, and he asked what movies she had been in, and I said none, she was much too good for a movie.

I didn't get to suggest phoning Lon Cohen to Wolfe because when he came down from the plant rooms at eleven o'clock I wasn't there. As I was finishing my second cup of coffee a phone call came from the District Attorney's office inviting me to drop in, and I went and spent a couple of hours at Leonard Street with an assistant DA named Brill. When we got through I knew slightly more than I had when we started, but he didn't. He had a copy of our statement on his desk, and what could I add to that? He had a lot of fun, though. He would pop a question at me and then spend nine minutes studying the statement to see if I had tripped.

Getting home a little before noon, I was prepared to find Wolfe grumpy. He likes me to be there when he comes down from the plant rooms to the office, and while he can't very well complain when the DA calls me on business that concerns us, this wasn't our affair. We had no client and no case and no fee in prospect. But I got a surprise. He wasn't grumpy; he was busy. He had the phone book open before him on his desk. He had actually gone to my desk, stooped to get the book, lifted it, and carried it around to his chair. Unheard of.

"Good morning," I said. "What's the emergency?"

"No emergency. I needed to know a number."

"Can I help?"

"Yes. I have instructions."

I sat. He wants you at his level because it's too much trouble to tilt his head back. "Nothing new," I said, "at the DA's office. Do you want a report?"

"No. You will go to Alec Gallant's place on Fifty-fourth Street and speak with Mr. Gallant, his sister, Miss Prince, Miss Thorne, and Mr. Drew. Separately if possible. You will tell each of them— You read the *Times* this morning as usual?"

"Certainly."

"You will tell each of them that I have engaged to make certain inquiries about Miss Sarah Yare, and that I shall be grateful for any information they may be able and willing to furnish. I would like to see any communications they may have received from her, say in the past month. Don't raise one brow like that. You know it disconcerts me."

"I've never seen you disconcerted yet." I let the brow down a little. "If they ask me who engaged you what do I say?"

"That you don't know. You are merely following instructions."

"If I ask you who engaged you what do you say?"

"I tell you the truth. No one. Or more accurately, I have engaged myself. I think I may have been hoodwinked and I intend to find out. You may be fishing where there are no fish. They may all say they have never had any association with Sarah Yare, and they may be telling the truth or they may not. You will have that in mind and form your conclusions. If any of them acknowledge association with her, pursue it enough to learn the degree of intimacy, but don't labor it. That can wait until we bait a hook. You are only to discover if there are any fish."

"Now?"

"Yes. The sooner the better."

I stood up. "It may take a while if the cops and the DA are working on them, and they probably are. How urgent is it? Do you want progress reports by phone?"

"Not unless you think it necessary. You must get all five of them."

"Right. Don't wait dinner for me." I went.

On the way uptown in the taxi I was using my brain. I will not explain at this point why Wolfe wanted to know if any of the subjects had known Sarah Yare, and if so how well, for two reasons: first, you have certainly spotted it yourself; and second, since I am not as smart as you are, I had not yet come up with the answer. It was underneath. On top, what I was using my brain for, was the phone book. Unquestionably it was connected with his being hoodwinked, since that was what was biting him, and therefore it probably had some bearing on the call that had been made from his office to Bianca Voss, but what could he accomplish by consulting the phone book? For that I had no decent guess, let alone an answer, by the time I paid the hackie at Fifty-fourth and Fifth Avenue.

Alec Gallant Incorporated, on the north side of the street near Madison Avenue, was no palace, either outside or in. The front was maybe thirty feet, and five feet of that was taken by the separate entrance to the side hall. The show window, all dark green, had just one exhibit: a couple of yards of plain black fabric, silk or rayon or nylon or Orlon or Dacron or cottonon or linenon, draped on a little rack. Inside, nothing whatever was in sight—that is, nothing to buy. The wall-to-wall carpet was the same dark green as the show window. There were mirrors and screens and tables and ashtrays, and a dozen or more chairs, not fancy, more to sit in than to look at. I had taken three steps on the carpet when a woman standing with a man by a table left him to come to meet me. I told her my name and said I would like to see Mr. Gallant. The man, approaching, spoke.

"Mr. Gallant is not available. What do you want?"

That didn't strike me as a very tactful greeting to a man who, for all he knew, might be set to pay eight hundred dollars for an afternoon frock, but of course he had had a tough twenty-four hours, so I kept it pleasant. "I'm not a reporter," I assured him, "or a cop, or a lawyer drumming up trade. I'm a private detective named Archie Goodwin, sent by a private detective named Nero Wolfe to ask Mr. Gallant a couple of harmless questions—not connected with the death of Bianca Voss."

174

"Mr. Gallant is not available."

I hadn't heard his voice in person before, only on the phone, but I recognized it. Also he looked like a business manager, with his neat well-arranged face, his neat well-made dark suit, and his neat shadow-stripe four-in-hand. He was a little puffy around the eyes, but the city and county employees had probably kept him from getting much sleep.

"May I ask," I asked, "if you are Mr. Carl Drew?"

"Yes. I am."

"Then I'm in luck. I was instructed to see five different people here—Mr. Gallant, Miss Gallant, Miss Prince, Miss Thorne, and Mr. Carl Drew. Perhaps we could sit down?"

He ignored that. "See us about what?"

The woman had left us. She was in earshot if her hearing was good, but this was certainly no secret mission, with five of them on the list. "To get information," I told him, "if you have any, about a woman who died yesterday. Not Bianca Voss. Miss Sarah Yare."

"Oh." He blinked. "Yes. That was tragic. Information? What kind of information?"

"I don't exactly know." I was apologetic. "All I know is that someone has engaged Mr. Wolfe to make inquiries about her, and he sent me to ask you people if you had any messages or letters from her in the past month or so, and if so will you let him see them."

"Messages or letters?"

"Right."

"That seems a little— Who engaged him?"

"I don't know." I was not permitting my face or voice to show that I had caught sight of a fish. "If you have had messages or letters, and would like to know who wants to see them before you produce them, I suppose Mr. Wolfe would tell you. He would have to."

"I have no messages or letters."

I was disappointed. "None at all? I said the past month or so, but before that would help. Any time."

He shook his head. "I never have had any. I doubt if she ever wrote a letter—that is, to anyone

175

here—or any messages, except phone messages. She always did everything by telephone. And for the past month, longer than that, more than a year, she hasn't been—uh—she hasn't been around."

"I know." I was sympathetic, and I meant it, though not for him. "Anyway, I don't think Mr. Wolfe would be interested in letters about clothes. I think it's personal letters he wants, and he thought you might have known her well enough personally to have some."

"Well, I haven't. I can't say I didn't know her personally—she was a very fine customer here for two years, and she was a very personal person. But I never had a personal letter from her."

I had to resist temptation. I had him talking, and there was no telling if or when I would get at the others. But Wolfe had said not to labor it, and I disobey instructions only when I have reason to think I know more about it than he does, and at that moment I didn't even know why he had been consulting the phone book. So I didn't press. I thanked him and said I would appreciate it if he would tell me when Mr. Gallant would be available. He said he would find out, and left me, going to the rear and disappearing around the end of a screen, and soon I heard his voice, but too faint to get any words. There was no other voice, so, being a detective, I figured it out that he was on a phone. That accomplished, I decided to detect whether the woman, who was seated at a table going through a portfolio, was either Anita Prince or Emmy Thorne. I voted no, arriving at it by a process so subtle and complicated that I won't go into it.

Drew reappeared, and I met him in the middle of the room. He said that Mr. Gallant was in his office with Miss Prince and could let me have five minutes. Another fish. Certainly Drew had told Gallant what my line was, and why did I rate even five seconds? As Drew led me to an elevator and entered with me, and pushed the button marked "2," I had to remember to look hopeful instead of smug.

The second-floor hall was narrow, with bare walls, and not carpeted. As I said, not a palace. After

176

following Drew down six paces and through a door, I found myself in a pin-up paradise. All available space on all four walls was covered with women, drawings and prints and photographs, both black-and-white and color, all sizes, and in one respect they were all alike: none of them had a stitch on. It hadn't occurred to me that a designer of women's clothes should understand female anatomy, but I admit it might help. The effect was so striking that it took me four or five seconds to focus on the man and woman seated at a table. By that time Drew had pronounced my name and gone.

Though the man and woman were fully clothed, they were striking too. He reminded me of someone, but I didn't remember who until later: Lord Byron—a picture of Lord Byron in a book in my father's library that had impressed me at an early age. It was chiefly Gallant's dark curly hair backing up a wide sweeping forehead, but the nose and chin were in it too. The necktie was all wrong; instead of Byron's choker he was sporting a narrow ribbon tied in a bow with long ends hanging.

The woman didn't go with him. She was small and trim, in a tailored suit that had been fitted by an expert, and her face was all eyes. Not that they popped, but they ran the show. In spite of Alec Gallant's lordly presence, as I approached the table I found myself aiming at Anita Prince's eyes.

Gallant was speaking. "What's this? About Sarah Yare?"

"Just a couple of questions." He had eyes too, when you looked at them. "It shouldn't take even five minutes. I suppose Mr. Drew told you?"

"He said Nero Wolfe is making an inquiry and sent you. What about? About how she died?"

"I don't think so, but I'm not sure. The fact is, Mr. Gallant, on this I'm just an errand boy. My instructions were to ask if you got any messages or letters from her in the past month or so, and if so will you let Mr. Wolfe see them."

"My God." He closed his eyes, tilted his head back, and shook it—a lion pestered by a fly. He looked at the woman. "This is too much. Too much!"

He looked at me. "You must know a woman was assassinated here yesterday. Of course you do!" He pointed at the door. "There!" His hand dropped to the desk like a dead bird. "And after that calamity, now this, the death of my old and valued friend. Miss Yare was not only my friend; in mold and frame she was perfection, in movement she was music, as a mannequin she would have been divine. My delight in her was completely pure. I never had a letter from her." His head jerked to Anita Prince. "Send him away," he muttered.

She put fingers on his arm. "You gave him five minutes, Alec, and he has only had two." Her voice was smooth and sure. The eyes came to me. "So you don't know the purpose of Mr. Wolfe's inquiry?"

"No, Miss Prince, I don't. He only tells me what he thinks I need to know."

"Nor who hired him to make it?"

So Drew had covered the ground. "No. Not that either. He'll probably tell you, if you have what he wants, letters from her, and you want to know why he wants to see them."

"I have no letters from her. I never had any. I had no personal relations with Miss Yare." Her lips smiled, but the eyes didn't. "Though I saw her many times, my contact with her was never close. Mr. Gallant preferred to fit her himself. I just looked on. It seems—" She stopped for a word, and found it. "It seems odd that Nero Wolfe should be starting an inquiry immediately after her death. Or did he start it before?"

"I couldn't say. The first I knew, he gave me this errand this morning. This noon."

"You don't know much, do you?"

"No, I just take orders."

"Of course you do know that Miss Yare committed suicide?"

I didn't get an answer in. Gallant, hitting the table with a palm, suddenly shouted at her, "Name of God! Must you? Send him away!"

"I'm sorry, Mr. Gallant," I told him. "I guess my

time's up. If you'll tell me where to find your sister and Miss Thorne, that will—"

I stopped because his hand had darted to an ashtray, a big metal one that looked heavy, and since he wasn't smoking he was presumably going to let fly with it. Anita Prince beat him to it. With her left hand she got his wrist, and with her right she got the ashtray and moved it out of reach. It was very quick and deft. Then she spoke, to me. "Miss Gallant is not here. Miss Thorne is busy, but you can ask Mr. Drew downstairs. You had better go."

I went. In more favorable circumstances I might have spared another five minutes for a survey of the pin-ups, but not then, not if I had to dodge ashtrays.

In the hall, having pulled the door shut, the indicated procedure, indicated both by the situation and by Miss Prince's suggestion, was to take the elevator down and see Drew again, but a detective is supposed to have initiative. So when I heard a voice, female, floating out through an open door, I went on past the elevator, to the door, for a look. Not only did I see, I was seen, and a voice, anything but female, came at me.

"You. Huh?"

I could have kicked myself. While, as I said, my mission couldn't be called secret with five people on the list, certainly Wolfe had intended it to be private, and there was Sergeant Purley Stebbins of Homicide West, glaring at me.

"Sightseeing?" he asked. Purley's idea of humor is a little primitive. "The scene of the crime?"

I descended to his level. "Just morbid," I told him, crossing the sill. "Compulsion neurosis. Is this it?"

Evidently it was. The room was about the same size as Alec Gallant's, but while his had been dominated by women without clothes, this one ran to clothes without women. There were coats, suits, dresses, everything. They were on dummies, scattered around; on hangers, strung on a pole along a wall; and piled on a table. At my right one dummy, wearing a skirt, was bare from the waist up; she might have blushed if she had had a face to blush with. There was one exception: a well-made tan wool dress standing by a corner of a desk contained a woman—a very attractive specimen in mold and frame, and in movement she could have been music. Standing beside her was Carl Drew. Seated at the desk was Sergeant Purley Stebbins, with a paper in his hand and other papers on the desk. Also on the desk, at his left, was a telephone—the one, presumably, that Wolfe and I had heard hit the floor.

What I had stumbled into was obvious. Purley was examining the effects, including papers, probably the second time over, of Bianca Voss, deceased, under surveillance on behalf of Alec Gallant Incorporated.

"Actually," I said, advancing past the immodest dummy, "this is one homicide I have no finger in. I'm on a fishing trip." I moved my eyes. "Would you tell me, Mr. Drew, where I can find Miss Thorne?"

"Right here," the tan wool dress said. "I am Miss Thorne."

"I'm Archie Goodwin of Nero Wolfe's office. May I have a word with you?"

She exchanged glances with Carl Drew. Her glance told me that Drew had told her about me; and his, if I am half as bright as I ought to be, told me that if he was not on a more personal basis with her than he had been with Sarah Yare it wasn't his fault. If he wasn't he would like to be.

"Go ahead," Drew told her. "I'll stick around." She moved toward the door, and I was following when Purley pronounced my name, my last name. He has on occasion called me Archie, but not when I suddenly appeared, uninvited, when he was working on a homicide. I turned.

"Who are you fishing for?" he demanded.

"If I knew," I said, "I might tell you, but don't hold your breath." There was no point in trying to sugar him. The damage, if any, had been done the second he saw me. "See you in court."

Emmy Thorne led me down the hall to a door, the next one, and opened it. Walking, she could have been music at that, if her heels had had any purchase.

She held the door for me to enter, shut it, went to a chair behind a desk, and sat. The room was less than half the size of the others and displayed neither women nor clothes.

"Sit down," she said. "What is this nonsense about letters from Sarah Yare?"

I took the chair at the end of her desk. "You know," I said, "my tie must be crooked or I've got a grease spot. Mr. Drew resented me, and Mr. Gallant was going to throw an ashtray at me. Now you. Why is it nonsense to ask a simple question politely and respectfully?"

"Maybe 'nonsense' isn't the word. Maybe I should have said 'gall.' What right have you to march in here and ask questions at all? Polite or not."

"None. It's not a right, it's a liberty. I have no right to ask you to have dinner with me this evening, which might not be a bad idea, but I'm at liberty to, and you're at liberty to tell me you'd rather dine at the automat with a baboon, only that wouldn't be very polite. Also when I ask if you have any letters from Sarah Yare you're at liberty to tell me to go climb a tree if you find the question ticklish. I might add that I would be at liberty to climb a pole instead of a tree. Have you any letters from Sarah Yare?"

She laughed. She had fine teeth. She stopped laughing abruptly. "Good Lord," she said, "I didn't think I would laugh for a year. This mess, what happened here yesterday, and then Sarah. No, I have no letters from her. You don't have to climb a tree." The laughter was all gone, and her gray eyes, straight at me, were cool and keen. "What else?"

Again I had to resist temptation. With Drew the temptation had been purely professional; with her it was only partly professional and only partly pure. Cramer had said she was in charge of contacts, and one more might be good for her.

Having resisted, I shook my head. "Nothing else, unless you know of something. For instance, if you know of anyone who might have letters."

"I don't." She regarded me. "Of course I'm curious, if you want to call it that. I was very fond of

Sarah, and this coming after all her trouble, naturally I'm wondering why you came here. You say Nero Wolfe is making an inquiry?"

"Yes, he sent me. I don't know who his client is, but my guess would be that it's some friend of Miss Yare's." I stood up. "Someone else may be curious. Thank you, Miss Thorne. I'm glad I don't have to climb a tree."

She got up and offered a hand. "You might tell me who it is."

"I might if I knew." Her hand was cool and firm and I kept it for a second. "I'm sorry I interrupted you in there." That was absolutely true. "By the way, one more liberty: is Miss Gallant around?"

She said no and came with me to the hall and left me, heading for the scene of the crime. I went the other way, to the elevator. Down on the main floor the woman was there alone, at a table with a portfolio. Not at all like Macy's main floor. Emerging, I turned left, found a phone booth on Madison Avenue, dialed the number I knew best, got Fritz, and asked for Wolfe.

His voice came. "Yes, Archie?"

"It's full of fish. Swarming. Sarah Yare bought her clothes there for two years and they all loved her. I'm phoning to ask about Flora Gallant. I've seen all the others, but Flora isn't around. My guess is that she's at the DA's office. Do I stick until she comes?"

"No. Satisfactory."

"Any further instructions?"

"No. Come home."

IV

In the office, after a late lunch of corned-beef hash with mushrooms, chicken livers, white wine, and grated cheese, which Fritz apologized for because he had had to keep it warm too long, I gave Wolfe a full report of the fishing trip, including all dialogue. When I had finished he nodded, took in air through his nose all the way down, and let it out through his mouth.

"Very well," he said, "that settles it. You will now go—"

"Just a minute," I cut in. "It doesn't settle it for me. It was bad enough up there, not knowing the score, and before I do any more going I want a little light. Why did you pick on Sarah Yare, and where did the phone book come in?"

"I have an errand for you."

"Yeah. Will it keep for ten minutes?"

"I suppose so."

"Then why?"

He leaned back. "As I told you this morning, I thought I might have been hoodwinked and I intended to find out. It was quite possible that that performance here yesterday—getting us on the phone just in time to hear a murder committed—was flummery. Indeed, it was more than possible. Must I expound that?"

"No. Even Cramer suspected it."

"So he did. But his theory that Bianca Voss had been killed earlier and that another woman, not the murderer, was there beside the corpse waiting for a phone call, was patently ridiculous. Must I expound that?"

"No, unless it was a lunatic. Anyone who would

do that, even the murderer, with the chance that someone might come in any second, would be batty."

"Of course. But if she wasn't killed at the time we heard those sounds she must have been killed earlier, since you phoned almost immediately and sent someone to that room. Therefore the sounds didn't come from there. Miss Gallant did not dial that number. She dialed the number of some other person whom she had persuaded to perform that hocus-pocus."

He turned a hand over. "I had come to that conclusion, or call it surmise, before I went to bed last night, and I had found it intolerable. I will not be mistaken for a jackass. Reading the *Times* at breakfast this morning, the item about the death of Sarah Yare, my attention was caught by the fact that she had been an actress. An actress can act a part. Also she had been in distress. Also she had died. If she had been persuaded to act *that* part, it would be extremely convenient—for the one who persuaded her—for her to die before she learned that a murder had been committed and she had been an accessory after the fact. Certainly that was mere speculation, but it was not idle, and when I came down to the office I looked in the phone book to see if Sarah Yare was listed, found that she was, and dialed her number. Algonquin nine, one-eight-four-seven."

"What for? She was dead."

"I didn't lift the receiver. I merely dialed it, to hear it. Before doing so I strained my memory. I had to recall an experience that was filed somewhere in my brain, having reached it through my ears. As you know, I am trained to attend, to observe, and to register. So are you. That same experience is filed in your brain. Close your eyes and find it. Take your ears back to yesterday, when you were standing there, having surrendered your chair to Miss Gallant, and she was at the phone, dialing. Not the first number she dialed; you dialed that one yourself later. The second one, when, according to her, she was dialing the number of the direct line to Bianca Voss's office. Close

184

your eyes and let your ears and brain take you back. Insist on it."

I did so. I got up and stood where I had stood while she was dialing, shut my eyes, and brought it back. In ten seconds I said, "Okay."

"Keep your eyes closed. I'm going to dial it. Compare."

The sound came of his dialing. I held my breath till the end, then opened my eyes and said positively, "No. Wrong. The first and third and fourth were wrong. The second might—"

"Close your eyes and try it again. This will be another number. Say when."

I shut my eyes and took five seconds. "Go."

The dialing sound came, the seven units. I opened my eyes. "That's more like it. That was it, anyway the first four. Beyond that I'm a little lost. But in that case—"

"Satisfactory. The first four were enough. The first number, which you rejected, as I did this morning, was Plaza two, nine-oh-two-two, the number of Bianca Voss's direct line according to the phone book —the number which Miss Gallant pretended to be dialing. The second was Sarah Yare's number, Algonquin nine, one-eight-four-seven."

"Well." I sat down. "I'll be damned."

"So it was still a plausible surmise, somewhat strengthened, but no more than that. If those people, especially Miss Gallant, could not be shown to have had some association with Sarah Yare, it was untenable. So I sent you to explore, and what you found promoted the surmise to an assumption, and a weighty one. What time is it?"

He would have had to twist his neck a whole quarter-turn to look at the wall clock, whereas I had only to lower my eyes to see my wrist. I obliged. "Five to four."

"Then instructions for your errand must be brief, and they can be. You will go to Sarah Yare's address on Thirteenth Street and look at her apartment. Her phone might have been discontinued since that book

185

was issued. I need to know that the instrument is still there and operable before I proceed. If I intend to see that whoever tried to make a fool of me regrets it, I must take care not to make a fool of myself. Have I furnished the light you wanted?"

I told him it was at least a glimmer and departed on the errand. If you think I might have shown fuller appreciation of his dialing display, I beg to differ. There is no point in assuring a man that he is a genius when he already knows it. Besides, I was too busy being sore at me. I should have thought of it myself. I certainly should have caught on when I saw him with the phone book.

It was not my day. At the address of the late Sarah Yare on East Thirteenth Street I stubbed my toe again. One thing I think I'm good at is sizing up people, and I was dead wrong about the janitor of that old walk-up. He looked as if anything would go, so I merely told him to let me into Sarah Yare's apartment to check the telephone, and the bum insisted on seeing my credentials. So I misjudged him again. I offered him a sawbuck and told him I only wanted two minutes for a look at the phone with him at my elbow, and when he turned me down I showed him a twenty. He just sneered at it. By that time we were bitter enemies, and if I had showed him a C he would probably have spit on it. The upshot was that I went back home for an assortment of keys, returned, posted myself across the street, waited nearly an hour to be sure the enemy was not peeking, and broke and entered, technically.

I won't describe it; it was too painful. It was a hell of a dump for a Sarah Yare, even for a down-and-outer who had once been Sarah Yare. But the telephone was there, and it was working. I dialed to make sure, and got Fritz, and told him I just wanted to say hello and would be home in fifteen minutes, and he said that would please Mr. Wolfe because Inspector Cramer was there.

"No," I said.

"Yes," he said.

"When did he come?"

"Ten minutes ago. At six o'clock. Mr. Wolfe said to admit him and is with him in the office. Hurry home, Archie."

I did so.

I got a hackie who liked to take advantages, and it took a little less than the fifteen minutes. I ascended the stoop and let myself in, not banging the door, and tiptoed down the hall and stopped short of the office door, thinking to get a sniff of the atmosphere before entering. I got it. Wolfe's voice came.

". . . and I didn't say I have never known you to be wrong, Mr. Cramer. I said I have never known you to be more wrong. That is putting it charitably, under provocation. You have accused me of duplicity. Pfui!"

"Nuts." Cramer had worked up to his grittiest rasp. "I have accused you of nothing. I have merely stated facts. The time of the murder was supposed to be established by you and Goodwin hearing it on the phone. Is that a fact? Those five people all have alibis for that time. One of them was here with you. Is that a fact? When I put it to you yesterday that that phone business might have been faked, that she might have been killed earlier, all I got was a runaround. You could challenge it circumstantially but not intrinsically, whatever the hell that means. Is that a fact? So that if you and Goodwin got to the witness stand you might both swear that you were absolutely satisfied that you had heard her get it at exactly half past eleven. Is that a fact? Giving me to understand that you weren't interested, you weren't concerned, you had no—"

"No," Wolfe objected. "That was not broached."

"Nuts. You know damn well it was implied. You said you had never had any association with any of those people besides what was in your statement, so how could you be concerned, with Bianca Voss dead? Tell me this, did any of them approach you, directly or indirectly, between seven o'clock yesterday and noon today?"

"No."

"But—" He bore down on the 'but.' "*But* you sent Goodwin there today. He told Stebbins he was on

187

a fishing trip. He talked with Drew, and Gallant, and Miss Prince, and he actually took Miss Thorne from under Stebbins' nose, took her out to talk with her. Is that a fact? And they all refused to tell what Goodwin said to them or what they said to him. That *is* a fact. They say it was a private matter and had nothing to do with the murder of Bianca Voss. And when I come and ask you what you sent Goodwin there for, ask you plainly and politely, you say that you will— What are you laughing at?"

It wasn't a laugh, I just barely caught it, it was hardly even a chuckle, but all the same it could get under your skin. I knew.

"It escaped me, Mr. Cramer. Your choice of adverbs. Your conception of politeness. Pray continue."

"All right, I asked you. And you said you will probably be ready to tell me within twenty-four hours. And what I said was absolutely justified. I did not accuse you of duplicity. You know what I said."

"I do indeed, Mr. Cramer." I couldn't see Wolfe, but I knew he had upturned a palm. "This is childish and futile. If a connection is established between your murder investigation and the topic of Mr. Goodwin's talks with those people today, it will be only because I formed a conjecture and acted on it. I hope to establish it within twenty-four hours, and meanwhile it will do no harm to give you a hint. Have you any information on the death of a woman named Sarah Yare?"

"Some, yes. Presumed a suicide, but it's being checked. I have two men on it. What about it?"

"I suggest that you assign more men to it, good ones, and explore it thoroughly. I think we will both find it helpful. I may soon have a more concrete suggestion, but for the present that should serve. You know quite well—"

The doorbell rang. I about-faced and looked through the one-way glass panel of the front door. It wasn't a visitor on the stoop, it was a mob. All five of them were there: Gallant, his sister, Anita Prince, Emmy Thorne, and Carl Drew. Fritz appeared from the kitchen, saw me, and stopped. I got my notebook and pen from pockets and wrote:

That phone works. The five subjects are outside wanting in.

AG

I told Fritz to stand by, tore out the sheet, entered the office and crossed to Wolfe's desk, and handed it to him.

Wolfe read it, frowned at it for three seconds, turned his head and called, "Fritz!"

Fritz appeared at the door. "Yes, sir?"

"Put the chain-bolt on and tell those people they will be admitted shortly. Stay there."

"Yes, sir." Fritz went.

Wolfe looked at Cramer. "Mr. Gallant, his sister, Miss Prince, Miss Thorne, and Mr. Drew have arrived, uninvited and unexpected. You'll have to leave without being seen. In the front room until they have entered. I'll communicate with you later."

"Like hell I'll leave." Cramer was on his feet. "Like hell they're unexpected." He was moving, toward the hall, his intention plain—taking over as receptionist.

"Mr. Cramer!" It snapped at his back, turning him. "Would I lie so clumsily? If they had been expected would I have let you in? Would I have sat here bickering with you? Either you leave or I do. If you admit them you'll have them to yourself, and I wish you luck."

Cramer was glaring. "You think I'm going to sneak out and sit on your goddam stoop until you whistle?"

"That *would* be unseemly," Wolfe conceded. "Very well." He pointed at a picture on the wall to his left behind him—a pretty waterfall. "You know about that. You may take that station, but only if you engage not to disclose yourself unless you are invited. Unequivocally."

The waterfall covered a hole in the wall. On the other side, in a wing of the hall across from the kitchen, the hole was covered by nothing, and you could not only see through but also hear through. Cramer had used it once before, a couple of years ago.

189

Cramer stood, considering. Wolfe demanded, "Well? They're waiting. For you or for me?"

Cramer said, "Okay, we'll try it your way," turned and marched to the hall, and turned left.

Wolfe told me, "All right, Archie. Bring them in."

V

Lord Byron, alias Alec Gallant, and the red leather chair went together fine. He sat well back, unlike most people I have seen there. Usually they are either too mad or too upset. Any of the other four probably would have been; they looked it. They were on yellow chairs that I had moved up to make a row facing Wolfe, with Emmy Thorne nearest me, then Anita Prince, then Carl Drew, then Flora Gallant. That put Flora nearest her brother, which seemed appropriate.

Wolfe was turned to Gallant. "You ask me, sir, why I sent Mr. Goodwin to ask you people about Sarah Yare. Of course I'm under no compulsion to reply, and I'm not sure that I am prepared to. Instead, I may ask why his questions, certainly not provocative, so disturbed you. Apparently they have even impelled you to call on me in a body. Why?"

"Talk," Gallant said. "*Vent*. Wind." There was an ashtray on the little table at his elbow, but not a heavy one.

Anita Prince put in, "The police have insisted on knowing why he was there, what he wanted."

Wolfe nodded. "And you refused to say. Why?"

"Because," Emmy Thorne declared, "it was none of their business. And we have a right to know why you sent him, whether his questions were provocative or not." That girl was strong on rights.

Wolfe's eyes went from right to left and back again. "There's no point," he said, "in dragging this out. I'll grant your question priority and we'll go on from there. I sent Mr. Goodwin to see you because I

191

suspected I had been gulled and wanted to find out; and further, because I had guessed that there was a connection between Sarah Yare, and her death, and the murder of Bianca Voss. By coming here en masse you have made that guess a conviction, if any doubt had remained."

"I knew it," Flora Gallant mumbled.

"*Tais-toi*," her brother commanded her. To Wolfe: "I'll tell you why we came here. We came for an explanation. We came—"

"For an understanding," Carl Drew cut in. "We're in trouble, all of us, you know that, and we need your help, and we're ready to pay for it. First we have to know what the connection is between Sarah Yare and what happened to Bianca Voss."

Wolfe shook his head. "You don't mean that. You mean you have to know whether I have established the connection, and if so, how. I'm willing to tell you, but before I do so I must clarify matters. There must be no misunderstanding. For instance, I understand that all of you thought yourselves gravely endangered by Miss Voss's presence. You, Miss Prince, you, Miss Thorne, and you, Mr. Drew— your dearest ambitions were threatened. Your future was committed to the success and glory of that enterprise, and you were convinced that Miss Voss was going to cheapen it, and perhaps destroy it. Do you challenge that?"

"Of course not." Emmy Thorne was scornful. "Everybody knew it."

"Then that's understood. That applies equally to you, Miss Gallant, but with special emphasis. You also had a more intimate concern, for your brother. You told me so. As for you, Mr. Gallant, you are not a man to truckle, yet you let that woman prevail. Presumably you were under severe constraint. Were you?"

Gallant opened his mouth and closed it. He looked at his sister, returned to Wolfe, and again opened his mouth and closed it. He was under constraint now, no doubt about that.

He forced it out. "I was under her heel." He

192

clamped his jaw. He unclamped it. "The police know. They found out enough, and I have told them the rest. She was a bad woman. I met her in France, during the war. We were in the Resistance together when I married her. Only afterward I learned that she was *perfide*. She had been a traitor to France—I couldn't prove it, but I knew it. I left her and changed my name and came to America—and then last year she found me and made demands. I was under her heel."

Wolfe grunted. "That won't do, Mr. Gallant. I doubt if it has satisfied the police, and it certainly doesn't satisfy me. In that situation you might have killed her, but surely you wouldn't have let her take charge of your business and your life. What else was there?"

"Nothing. Nothing!"

"Pfui. Of course there was. And if the investigation is prolonged the police will discover it. I advise you to disclose it and let me get on and settle this affair. Didn't her death remove her heel?"

"Yes. Thank God, it did." Gallant hit the arms of the chair with his palms. "With her gone there is no evidence to fear. She had two brothers, and they, like her, were traitors, and I killed them. I would have killed her too, but she escaped me. During the war it would have been merely an episode, but it was later, much later, when I found out about them, and by then it was a crime. With her evidence I was an *assassin*, and I was doomed. Now she is gone, thank God, but I did not kill her. You know I did not. At half past eleven yesterday morning I was in my workshop with Miss Prince and many others, and you can swear that she was killed at that moment. That is why we came to see you, to arrange to pay—"

"Hold it, Alec." Anita Prince headed him off. "Mr. Wolfe wants to clarify matters. Let him."

"The cat's head is out," Wolfe told her, "but I had already heard it scratch. Let's get on. I cannot swear that Bianca Voss was killed 'at that moment.' On the contrary, I'm sure she wasn't, for a variety of reasons. There are such minor ones as the extraordinary billingsgate she spat at me on the phone, quite

193

gratuitous; and her calling me a gob of fat. A woman who still spoke the language with so marked an accent would not have the word 'gob' so ready, and probably wouldn't have it at all."

He waved "gob" away. "But the major reasons are more cogent. In the first place, it was too pat. Since the complexities of nature permit a myriad of coincidences we cannot reject one offhand, but we can discriminate. That one—that the attack had come just at the moment when Miss Gallant had got Mr. Goodwin and me on the phone with her, was highly suspect. Besides, it was indiscreet to strike just then. Why not wait until she had hung up? Whoever was talking with her would certainly hear the sounds and take alarm. As I told Mr. Cramer, it was open to challenge circumstantially, though not intrinsically. However, there was another challenge, on surer ground. Miss Gallant did not dial Plaza two, nine-oh-two-two, Miss Voss's number, as she pretended. She dialed Algonquin nine, one-eight-four-seven, Sarah Yare's number."

A noise, a sort of low growl, came from the waterfall. I was farthest away, and I heard it distinctly, so it must have reached their ears too, but Wolfe's last words had so riveted their attention that it didn't register.

It did with Wolfe, and he added hastily, "I didn't know that yesterday. I became certain of it only after you rang my doorbell, when Mr. Goodwin handed me this note." He tapped it, there on his desk. "Its first words are 'That phone works.' I had sent him to learn if Sarah Yare's phone was in operation. Obviously, Miss Gallant had arranged with Miss Yare to impersonate Bianca Voss, and it is a reasonable—"

"Wait a minute." Gallant had come forward in the red leather chair. "You can't prove that."

"Directly, no. Inferentially, yes."

"And how do you know she dialed Sarah Yare's number? You weren't where you could see the dial, and neither was Goodwin."

Wolfe nodded. "Evidently you have discussed it with her. You're quite right, Mr. Gallant; we couldn't

194

see the dial. Nevertheless, we can supply evidence, and we think it will be persuasive. I am not—"

"What kind of evidence?"

"That's no good, Alec." It was Emmy Thorne, the contact girl. "You can't push Nero Wolfe. He has his teeth in it, you can see that. You know what we decided."

"I'm not sure," Anita Prince objected, "that we decided right."

"I am. Carl?"

"Yes." Drew was chewing his lip. "I think so. Yes."

"Flora? It's up to you."

"I guess so." Flora's voice was cracked, and she tried again. "I guess so." A little better.

Emmy nodded. "Go ahead, Alec. You can't push him."

"My God." Gallant looked at his sister, and back at Wolfe. "All right. We will pay you to help us. I will pay you. My sister is innocent and she must not suffer. It would be an offense against nature, against God Himself. She has told me all about it, and she was stupid, but she is innocent. She did arrange with Sarah Yare, as you said, but only to move you. She had read much about you and had a great opinion of your abilities. She was desperate about Bianca Voss. She knew you demanded high fees, much beyond her resources, so she conceived a plan. She would persuade you to talk with Bianca Voss on the phone, and she would get Sarah instead, and Sarah would abuse you with such violence that you would be offended and resent it, and you would be moved to act against Bianca Voss. It was stupid, yes, very stupid, but it was not criminal."

Wolfe's eyes, at him, were half closed. "And you want to pay me to help her."

"Yes. When I told her you had sent your man to inquire about Sarah Yare I saw she was frightened and asked her why, and she told me. I consulted the others, and it was apparent that you knew something, and that was dangerous. We decided to come and ask you to help. My sister must not suffer."

Wolfe's eyes moved. "Miss Gallant. You heard your brother. Did he quote you correctly?"

"Yes!" That time it was too loud.

"You did those things? As he related them?"

"Yes!"

Wolfe returned to Gallant. "I agree with you, sir, that your sister was stupid, but you are not the one to proclaim it. You say that she arranged with Sarah Yare to abuse me on the phone, but Miss Yare didn't stop at that. She ended by making noises indicating that she had been violently attacked, and jerked the phone off onto the floor, and made other noises, and then hung up the phone and cut the connection. Was that on her own initiative? Her own idea? Your sister's stupidity can bow to yours if you expected me to overlook that point—or worse, if you missed it yourself."

"I am not stupid, Mr. Wolfe."

"Then you are devious beyond my experience."

"Devious?"

"*Rusé. Subtil.*"

"No. I am not." Gallant clamped his jaw. He released it. "*Bien.* Suppose, only to suppose, she arranged that too, that comedy. Suppose even that she killed Bianca Voss. Was that a crime? No; it was justice; it was the hand of God. Bianca Voss was an evil woman. She was *vilaine.* Are you so virtuous that you must crucify my sister? Are you a paragon? For she is in your hands, at your mercy. You know about Sarah Yare, but the police do not. You know she dialed that number, but the police do not, and they will not unless you tell them. By your word it can be that my sister was here with you at the time that Bianca Voss was killed. As I have said, I will pay you. It will be a great service from you, and it deserves payment. I will trust you. I will pay you now."

Wolfe grunted. "That was quite a speech."

"It was not a speech. I do not make speeches. It was an appeal to your charity. From my heart."

"And to my cupidity." Wolfe shook his head. "No. I am not a paragon. I am not even a steward of the law. But you have ignored two important factors: one, my self-esteem. Even if Bianca Voss deserved to die, I will not permit a murderer to take me for a simpleton. Two, another woman died too. Was Sarah Yare also evil? Was she *vilaine?*"

"But she—Sarah killed herself!"

"No. I don't believe it. That's another coincidence I reject. Granted that she may have been wretched enough for that extreme, why did she choose that particular moment? Again too pat. According to the published account, she died between ten o'clock yesterday morning and two in the afternoon, but I can narrow it a little. Since she spoke with me on the phone at eleven-thirty, she died between that hour and two o'clock. I believe that the person who killed Bianca Voss at some time prior to eleven-thirty, and arranged with Sarah Yare to enact that comedy, as you call it, went to Sarah Yare's apartment later and killed her. Indeed, prudence demanded it. So you ask too much of my charity. If only Bianca Voss had died—"

"No!" Gallant exploded. "Impossible! Totally impossible! My sister loved Sarah! She killed her? Insane!"

"But you believe she killed Bianca Voss. You came here believing that. That was stupid too. She didn't."

Gallant gawked at him. Lord Byron shouldn't gawk, but he did. So did the others. Also they made noises. Carl Drew demanded, "Didn't? You say she *didn't?*" Emmy Thorne asked coolly, "What's this, Mr. Wolfe? A game?"

"No, madam, not a game. Nor a comedy—Mr. Gallant's word. As a man I know said yesterday, murder is no joke." Wolfe's eyes went to Flora. "There was much against you, Miss Gallant, especially the fact that you dialed that other number before you dialed Sarah Yare's, and asked someone you called Doris if Miss Voss was around. Are you too rattled to remember that?"

"No." She was clutching the rim of her bag with both hands. "I remember."

"Of course the reason for it was obvious, if you had killed Bianca Voss before you came here; you had to know that the body had not been found before you

197

proceeded with your stratagem. Since you had *not* killed Bianca Voss, why did you make that call?"

"I wanted to make sure that she hadn't gone out. That she was there in her office. You might call her again after I left and find out she hadn't been there. I didn't care if you called her and she denied she had talked to you like that. I thought you would think she was lying. I suppose that was stupid." Her mouth worked. "How did you know I didn't kill her?"

"You told me. You showed me. If you had devised that elaborate humbug, certainly you would have decided how to act at the moment of crisis. You would have decided to be alarmed, and shocked, and even perhaps a little dazed. But it wasn't like that. You were utterly stunned with bewilderment. When Mr. Goodwin told us what Mr. Drew had said, what did you say? You said, 'But how—' And repeated it, 'But how—' If you had killed Bianca Voss you would have had to be a master dramatist to write such a line, and an actress of genius to deliver it as you did; and you are neither."

Wolfe waved it away. "But that was for me. For others, for a judge and jury, I must do better, and I think I can. If you are innocent, someone else is guilty. Someone else learned of the arrangement you had made with Sarah Yare, either from you or from her, and persuaded her to add a dramatic climax. Someone else killed Bianca Voss and then established an invulnerable alibi for the crucial period. Someone else had secured the required amount of cyanide—it doesn't take much. Someone else, having established the alibi, went to Sarah Yare's apartment and poisoned her glass of whisky. That was done before two o'clock, and that should make it simple. Indeed, it *has* made it simple. Shortly before you came I learned from Mr. Cramer of the police that you arrived at your brother's place yesterday a few minutes after noon. Since you left here at a quarter of twelve, you hadn't had time to go first to Thirteenth Street and dispose of Sarah Yare; and you were continuously under the eyes of policemen the rest of the afternoon. That is correct?"

"Yes." Flora's eyes were wet but she hadn't used a handkerchief. "I wanted to go and see what had happened to Sarah, but I was afraid—I didn't know—"

"It's a good thing you didn't, madam. I also learned from Mr. Cramer that you, Mr. Gallant, you, Mr. Drew, and you, Miss Prince, were also constantly under surveillance, for hours, from the time the police arrived. That leaves you, Miss Thorne." His eyes were narrowed at her. "You were with three men in an office on Forty-sixth Street from eleven-twenty until a quarter to twelve. You arrived at Mr. Gallant's place, and found the police there, shortly before three o'clock. You may be able to account for the interim satisfactorily. Do you want to try?"

"I don't have to try." Emmy Thorne's gray eyes were not as cool and keen as they had been when she had told me I didn't have to climb a tree. She had to blink to keep them at Wolfe. "So it *is* a game."

"Not one you'll enjoy, I fear. Nor will I; I'm out of it now. To disclose your acquisition of the cyanide you would need for Sarah Yare; to show that you entered Bianca Voss's room yesterday morning, or could have, before you left for your business appointment; to find evidence of your visit to Thirteenth Street after your business appointment; to decide which homicide you will be put on trial for—all that is for others. You must see now that it was a mistake—*Archie!*"

I was up and moving, but halted. Gallant, out of his chair and advancing, wasn't going to touch her. His fists were doubled, but not to swing; they were pressed against his chest. He stopped square in front of her and commanded, "Look at me, Emmy."

To do so she would have had to move her head, tilt it back, and she moved nothing.

"I have loved you," he said. "Did you kill Sarah?"

Her lips moved but no sound came.

His fists opened for his fingers to spread on his chest. "So you heard us that day, and you knew I couldn't marry you because I was married to her, and you killed her. That I can understand, for I loved you. But that you killed Sarah, no. No! And even that is not the worst! Today, when I told you and the others

199

what Flora had told me, you accepted it, you allowed us to accept it, that she had killed Bianca. You would have let her suffer for it. Look at me! You would have let my sister—"

Flora was there, tugging at his sleeve, sputtering at him, "You love her, Alec, don't hurt her now, don't—"

Gallant jerked loose, backed up, folded his arms, and breathed; and Emmy Thorne moved. She came up out of her chair, stood rigid long enough to give Gallant a straight, hard look, shook her head, spun away from him, and headed for the door, brushing against Flora. Her route took her past Anita Prince, who tilted her head back to look up at her, and past Carl Drew, who had to pull his feet back not to trip her.

I didn't budge, thinking I wasn't needed, and I was right. In movement she might have been music, but if so, the music got stopped. As she made the hall and turned toward the front a hand gripped her arm —a hand that had had plenty of practice gripping arms.

"Take it easy, Miss Thorne," Cramer said. "We'll have to have a talk."

"*Grand Dieu,*" Gallant groaned, and covered his face with his hands.

ABOUT THE AUTHOR

REX STOUT, the creator of Nero Wolfe, was born in Noblesville, Indiana, in 1886, the sixth of nine children of John and Lucetta Todhunter Stout, both Quakers. Shortly after his birth, the family moved to Wakarusa, Kansas. He was educated in a country school, but, by the age of nine, was recognized throughout the state as a prodigy in arithmetic. Mr. Stout briefly attended the University of Kansas, but left to enlist in the Navy, and spent the next two years as a warrant officer on board President Theodore Roosevelt's yacht. When he left the Navy in 1908, Rex Stout began to write freelance articles, worked as a sightseeing guide and as an itinerant bookkeeper. Later he devised and implemented a school banking system which was installed in four hundred cities and towns throughout the country. In 1927 Mr. Stout retired from the world of finance and, with the proceeds of his banking scheme, left for Paris to write serious fiction. He wrote three novels that received favorable reviews before turning to detective fiction. His first Nero Wolfe novel, *Fer-de-Lance*, appeared in 1934. It was followed by many others, among them, *Too Many Cooks, The Silent Speaker, If Death Ever Slept, The Doorbell Rang* and *Please Pass the Guilt,* which established Nero Wolfe as a leading character on a par with Erle Stanley Gardner's famous protagonist, Perry Mason. During World War II, Rex Stout waged a personal campaign against Nazism as chairman of the War Writers' Board, master of ceremonies of the radio program "Speaking of Liberty" and as a member of several national committees. After the war, he turned his attention to mobilizing public opinion against the wartime use of thermonuclear devices, was an active leader in the Authors' Guild and resumed writing his Nero Wolfe novels. All together, his Nero Wolfe novels have been translated into twenty-two languages and have sold more than forty-five million copies. Rex Stout died in 1975 at the age of eighty-eight. A month before his death, he published his forty-sixth Nero Wolfe novel, *A Family Affair.*

REX STOUT
&
NERO WOLFE

Rex Stout created Nero Wolfe, that Falstaff in girth and wit, that serious eater, devoted orchidologist and acknowledged agoraphobe. Nero solved crimes by sheer brain-power and with more than a little help from the brash but efficient Archie Goodwin.

Nero Wolfe made his dazzling debut in 1934, when his creator was 47 years of age. And from then on the 286 pound, sedentary sleuth triumphed over a variety of evil forces that even included the F.B.I. Wolfe accomplished these feats between beers in a brownstone on West 35th Street in New York. Dispensing with crime laboratories and the like, he relied on old-fashioned logic of the sort practiced by Sherlock Holmes (the vowels in whose name were identical to Nero Wolfe's, even in their order).

Mr. Stout's Nero Wolfe books have appeared in over 22 languages and have sold more than forty-five million copies. Mr. Stout had completed forty-six mysteries starring Wolfe at the time of his death at 88. The first was *Fer de Lance,* the last *A Family Affair.* In between, there were forty-four other mysteries, each one of them a brilliant display of the talents of Rex Stout and the expert sleuth Nero Wolfe.

Bantam is currently bringing back into print one Rex Stout each month. The first books selected are: *And Be A Villain, The Golden Spiders, A Right To Die, A Family Affair, Trio For Blunt Instruments* and *Trouble In Triplicate.* Rex Stout books will be available wherever paperbacks are sold.